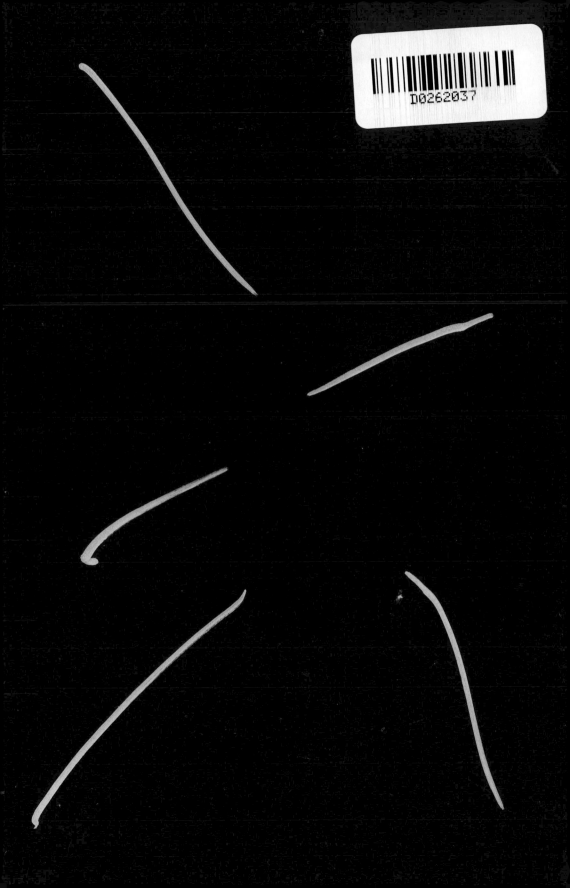

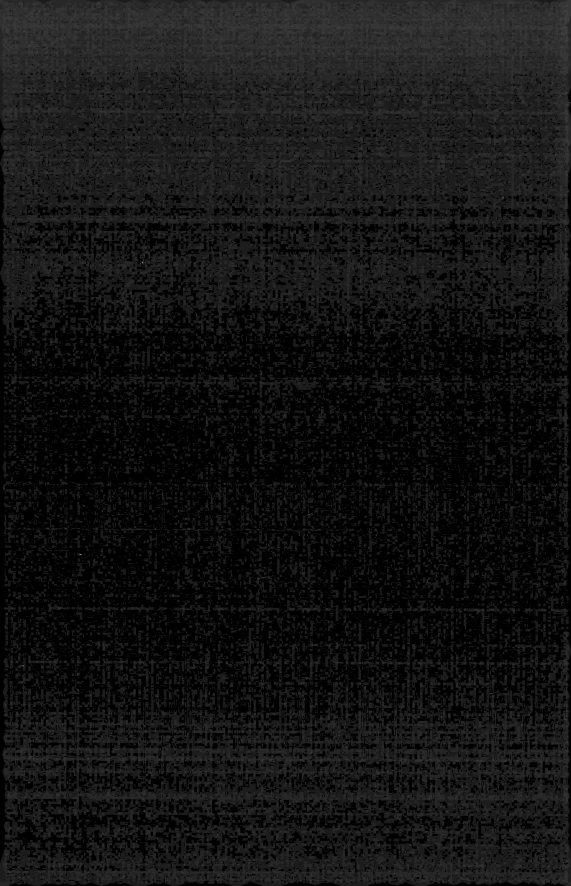

The
Young
Oxford Book
— of —
Nightmares

The
Young
Oxford Book
of
Nightmares

DENNIS PEPPER

UNIVERSITY PRESS

OXFORD

UNIVERSITY PRESS

Great Clarendon Street, Oxford OX2 6DP

Oxford University Press is a department of the University of Oxford.
It furthers the University's objective of excellence in research, scholarship,
and education by publishing worldwide in

Oxford New York

Athens Auckland Bangkok Bogotá Buenos Aires Calcutta
Cape Town Chennai Dar es Salaam Delhi Florence Hong Kong Istanbul
Karachi Kuala Lumpur Madrid Melbourne Mexico City Mumbai
Nairobi Paris São Paulo Singapore Taipei Tokyo Toronto Warsaw

with associated companies in Berlin Ibadan

Oxford is a registered trade mark of Oxford University Press
in the UK and in certain other countries

British Library Cataloguing in Publication Data available

ISBN 0-19-278179-0

1 3 5 7 9 10 8 6 4 2

Typeset by
Mike Brain Graphic Design Limited, Oxford

Printed and bound in Great Britain by Biddles Ltd
www.biddles.co.uk

Contents

Contents

Introduction

Nightmares are terrifying, but the link with our waking lives may be quite simple: we've eaten too much, or the cat's gone to sleep on top of us, or a loose sheet is lying across our neck. Sometimes, though, there seems to be no such direct link, no easy explanation, and then we begin to worry about what the nightmares may *mean*.

Writers seek explanations. They need to give significance to what they write about, and the nightmare is worked out in the 'real' lives of their characters. In this book you will find nightmares that have no simple explanation: nightmares that do not end when the dreamer wakes, nightmares through which the dead manage to communicate with the living, nightmares in which the dreamers know, without doubt, that they are trapped in a horrific situation that is outside their control or influence, nightmares in which it is uncertain what is real and what is not. You will find others, too.

As well as those nightmares most of us have experienced while we sleep, there are occasions in our waking lives that seem so awful that we can only describe them as 'nightmarish'. In Christopher Leach's story we have both the young man's nightmare experience of Greg's horrific death and the nightmare situation he finds himself in as the grim villagers enter Mrs Beale's kitchen. Juliet, in Kenneth Ireland's story, may awaken clawed and bleeding from her nightmare about the dead cat, but her real horror lies in her knowing what will happen when her parents leave and close her bedroom door behind them. Annie's nightmare, in Sheila Lavelle's comic story, used to wake her up sweating and groaning and with her heart banging, but that was before her real life nightmare when she performed her Scottish melody in the holiday camp talent competition.

A collection of nightmare stories, then, to put you off going to sleep at night. I've tried, as in earlier anthologies in this series, to bring together stories that you are unlikely to have read before. Some will certainly be new to you: those by Francis Beckett, Michael Chislett, Adèle Geras, John Gordon, Dennis Hamley, Kenneth Ireland, Sheila Lavelle, Alison Prince, Sue Welford, and Robert Scott were written for this book.

Pleasant dreams.

Dennis Pepper
March 2000

Mason's Life

KINGSLEY AMIS

M ay I join you?'
The medium-sized man with the undistinguished clothes and the blank, anonymous face looked up at Pettigrew, who, glass of beer in hand, stood facing him across the small corner table. Pettigrew, tall, handsome and of fully moulded features, had about him an intent, almost excited air that, in different circumstances, might have brought an unfavourable response, but the other said amiably, 'By all means. Do sit down.'

'Can I get you something?'

'No, I'm fine, thank you,' said the medium-sized man, gesturing at the almost full glass in front of him. In the background was the ordinary ambience of bar, barman, drinkers in ones and twos, nothing to catch the eye.

'We've never met, have we?'

'Not as far as I recall.'

'Good, good. My name's Pettigrew, Daniel R. Pettigrew. What's yours?'

'Mason. George Herbert Mason, if you want it in full.'

'Well, I think that's best, don't you? George . . . Herbert . . . Mason.' Pettigrew spoke as if committing the three short words to memory. 'Now let's have your telephone number.'

Again Mason might have reacted against Pettigrew's demanding manner, but he said no more than, 'You can find me in the book easily enough.'

'No, there might be several. . . . We mustn't waste time. Please.'

'Oh, very well; it's public information, after all. Two-three-two, five—'

'Hold on, you're going too fast for me. Two . . . three . . . two . . .'

'Five-four-five-four.'

'What a stroke of luck. I ought to be able to remember that.'

'Why don't you write it down if it's so important to you?'

At this, Pettigrew gave a knowing grin that faded into a look of disappointment. 'Don't you know that's no use? Anyway: two-three-two, five-four-five-four. I might as well give you my number too. Seven—'

'I don't want your number, Mr Pettigrew,' said Mason, sounding a little impatient, 'and I must say I rather regret giving you mine.'

'But you must take my number.'

'Nonsense; you can't make me.'

'A phrase, then—let's agree on a phrase to exchange in the morning.'

'Would you mind telling me what all this is about?'

'Please, our time's running out.'

'You keep saying that. This is getting—'

'Any moment everything might change and I might find myself somewhere completely different, and so might you, I suppose, though I can't help feeling it's doubtful whether—'

'Mr Pettigrew, either you explain yourself at once or I have you removed.'

'All right,' said Pettigrew, whose disappointed look had deepened, 'but I'm afraid it won't do any good. You see, when we started talking I thought you must be a real person, because of the way you—'

'Spare me your infantile catch-phrases, for heaven's sake. So I'm not a real person,' cooed Mason offensively.

'I don't mean it like that, I mean it in the most literal way possible.'

'Oh, God. Are you mad or drunk or what?'

'Nothing like that. I'm asleep.'

'Asleep?' Mason's nondescript face showed total incredulity.

'Yes. As I was saying, at first I took you for another real person in the same situation as myself: sound asleep, dreaming, aware of the fact, and anxious to exchange names and telephone numbers and so forth with the object of getting in touch the next day and confirming the shared experience. That would prove something remarkable about the mind, wouldn't it?— people communicating via their dreams. It's a pity one so seldom realizes one's dreaming: I've only been able to try the experiment four or five times in the last twenty years, and I've never had any success. Either I forget the details or I find there's no such person, as in this case. But I'll go on—'

'You're sick.'

'Oh no. Of course it's conceivable there is such a person as you. Unlikely, though, or you'd have recognized the true situation at once, I feel, instead of arguing against it like this. As I say, I may be wrong.'

'It's hopeful that you say that.' Mason had calmed down, and lit a cigarette with deliberation. 'I don't know much about these things, but you can't be too far gone if you admit you could be in error. Now let me just assure you that I didn't come into existence five minutes ago inside your head. My name, as I told you, is George Herbert Mason. I'm forty-six years old, married, three children, job in the furniture business . . . Oh hell, giving you no more than an outline of my life so far would take all night, as it would in the case of anybody with an average memory. Let's finish our drinks and go along to my house, and then we can—'

'You're just a man in my dream saying that,' said Pettigrew loudly. 'Two-three-two, five-four-five-four. I'll call the number if it exists, but it won't be you at the other end. Two-three-two—'

'Why are you so agitated, Mr Pettigrew?'

'Because of what's going to happen to you at any moment.'

'What . . . Is this a threat?'

Pettigrew was breathing fast. His finely drawn face began to coarsen, the pattern of his tweed jacket to become blurred. 'The telephone!' he shouted. 'It must be later than I thought!'

'Telephone?' repeated Mason, blinking and screwing up his eyes as Pettigrew's form continued to change.

'The one at my bedside! I'm waking up!'

Mason grabbed the other by the arm, but that arm had lost the greater part of its outline, had become a vague patch of light already fading, and when Mason looked at the hand that had done the grabbing, his own hand, he saw with difficulty that it likewise no longer had fingers, or front or back, or skin, or anything at all.

Seafood

FRANCIS BECKETT

They came onto the little beach warily, in small clusters, looking around them as though they feared attack at any moment. They were dressed raggedly: an old woman wore a tattered sheet that had once been white; a few had shorts on; some, especially the children, were naked.

Slowly they gathered in the middle of the little beach. They seemed to be debating what to do next, looking fearfully around them in the bright sunshine as the gentle waves lapped at their feet.

Suddenly the quiet sea boiled, and a dozen grey heads—the heads of dolphins—shot out of the sea, arranged in a semicircle. One of the women saw them, and Arkee saw her mouth open as she shouted a warning. They started to run, but the trap had been set. A huge net rose up from its hiding place beneath the sand and closed around them. The dolphins sank beneath the waves as fast as they had appeared, placed their grey heads inside the other end of the net, and swam out to sea, pulling the net with its screaming, struggling human cargo further and further out, then down beneath the waves.

As he watched them sink despairingly beneath the waves, Arkee tried to scream, but found that he could not make a sound. He tried again, and slowly realized that he was lying, hot and shivering, staring upwards in terror, and his mother's concerned face was above him, saying: 'It's all right, Mummy's here.' He opened his eyes, but took a few moments to realize where he was. Even then he could not get the image out of his mind, or the terrible screams, which he had not heard, but which he knew were there.

Arkee's mother was wise. She waited until she was sure he had come to himself, then said in a quiet, clear voice: 'It was just a dream. Do you want to tell me about it?'

He said nothing for a long, long time. Even then he did not answer the question. He just said: 'Is it true that humans used to rule the earth?'

Arkee's mother knew better than to say something silly like, 'What put that thought into your head?' She just answered, as best she could, the question her son had asked. It wasn't easy, because she didn't know the answer herself, but she said:

'I think so, darling. It was a long time ago. My grandfather used to tell me of a time, long ago . . . but it may have been a myth. Even he couldn't remember for sure.'

'What happened to . . . to change things?'

Arkee's mother sighed. She was tired—he had woken her from her own sleep—but she did not want to leave him unhappy or uncertain. Besides, it was time he knew.

'I think,' she said, 'that the air became poisonous, and the sun hotter. We don't know why, but my grandfather said he thought that the machines they built to take them from place to place made some sort of poisonous gas. Anyway, whatever caused it, everything that grew in the earth or walked on the land began to die. A few humans managed to survive, by living underground, but when they came out again—well, the land was dead and most of the things that had lived or grown on it were dead too. There was nothing left worth ruling over. That's the story, anyway.'

'And the sea?' said Arkee. 'Wasn't that poisoned too?'

'The sea managed better than the land. Fishes survived—in fact, my grandfather said there are more fishes than before, though we don't know why. Dolphins and other sea mammals adapted, spending more time under the sea and less time in the poisonous air. Dolphins developed a lot of new skills. Dolphins', she added, 'are highly intelligent.'

Arkee lay silent for a long while, and his mother was just starting to think that she might be able to get back to sleep herself when he said, so quietly she had to strain to hear him: 'It's cruel.'

There was an edge to his mother's voice now. 'Arkee, you mustn't think about it. There's nothing to be done . . .'

'The screams . . .'

'You mustn't.' She knew now, at least in part, what he had seen, and drew a deep breath and started to explain. 'Listen, Arkee. It's my fault for telling you about food harvesting yesterday. Creatures live by eating other creatures. I know it seems harsh and cruel. But that's the way it is. Sleep, my darling. Try to sleep.' But Arkee lay awake for a long, long time, and his mother stayed with him.

At last she moved quietly away, but she whispered before she went: 'Other creatures are often highly intelligent, but you mustn't think about them as though they could think and feel just like us. They can't. Believe me. Goodnight, darling.' And slowly the sharpness of the image in Arkee's head faded, and he began to feel calm and happy again, and turned over and yawned. His last thought, as he stared down his long grey snout at his gently flapping tail and felt the comforting mass of the seawater on his body, was that he was tired of eating fish. With any luck there would be human on his salted seaweed for breakfast tomorrow.

Nightmare in Blue

FREDRIC BROWN

He awoke to the brightest, bluest morning he had ever seen. Through the window beside the bed, he could see an almost incredible sky. George slid out of bed quickly, wide awake and not wanting to miss another minute of the first day of his vacation. But he dressed quietly so as not to awaken his wife. They had arrived here at the lodge—loaned them by a friend for the week of their vacation—late the evening before and Wilma had been very tired from the trip; he'd let her sleep as long as she could. He carried his shoes into the living room to put them on.

Tousle-haired little Tommy, their five year old, came out of the smaller bedroom he'd slept in, yawning. 'Want some breakfast?' George asked him. And when Tommy nodded, 'Get dressed then, and join me in the kitchen.'

George went to the kitchen but before starting breakfast, he stepped through the outside door and stood looking around; it had been dark when they'd arrived and he knew what the country was like only by description. It was virgin woodland, more beautiful than he'd pictured it. The nearest other lodge, he'd been told, was a mile away, on the other side of a fairly large lake. He couldn't see the lake for the trees but the path that started here from the kitchen door led to it, a little less than a quarter of a mile away. His friend had told him it was good for swimming, good for fishing. The swimming didn't interest George; he wasn't afraid of the water but he didn't like it either, and he'd never learned how to swim. But his wife was a good swimmer and so was Tommy—a regular little water rat, she called him.

Tommy joined him on the step; the boy's idea of getting dressed had been to put on a pair of swim trunks so that it hadn't taken him long. 'Daddy,' he said, 'let's go see the lake before we eat, huh, Daddy?'

'All right,' George said. He wasn't hungry himself and maybe when they got back Wilma would be awake.

The lake was beautiful, an even more intense blue than the sky, and smooth as a mirror. Tommy plunged into it gleefully and George called to him to stay where it was shallow, not to swim out.

'I can swim, Daddy. I swim swell.'

'Yes, but your mother's not here. You stay close.'

'Water's *warm*, Daddy.'

Far out, George saw a fish jump. Right after breakfast he'd come down with his rod and see if he could catch a lunch for them.

A path along the edge of the lake led, he'd been told, to a place a couple of miles away where rowboats could be rented; he'd rent one for the whole week and keep it tied up here. He stared towards the end of the lake trying to see the place.

Suddenly, chillingly, there was an anguished cry, '*Daddy, my leg, it—*'

George whirled and saw Tommy's head way out, twenty yards at least, and it went under the water and came up again, but this time there was a frightening *glubbing* sound when Tommy tried to yell again. It must be a cramp, George thought frantically; he'd seen Tommy swim several times that distance.

For a second he almost flung himself into the water, but then he told himself: It won't help him for me to drown with him and if I can get Wilma there's at least a chance . . .

He ran back towards the lodge. A hundred yards away he started yelling '*Wilma!*' at the top of his voice and when he was almost to the kitchen door she came through it, in pyjamas. And then she was running after him towards the lake, passing him and getting ahead since he was already winded, and he was fifty yards behind her when she reached the edge, ran into the water and swam strongly towards the spot where for a moment the back of the boy's head showed at the surface.

She was there in a few strokes and had him and then, as she put her feet down to tread water for the turn, he saw with sudden sheer horror—a horror mirrored in his wife's blue eyes—that she was standing on the bottom, holding their dead son, in only three feet of water.

Dream Ghost

SYDNEY J. BOUNDS

Mandy awoke suddenly in the night, trembling with fear. Moonlight flooded her bedroom with silver and shadow. It was only a dream, she told herself, only a dream. So why was she shivering in a warm bed?

A memory of the dream returned and she threw back the bedclothes and switched on the light. It had all seemed so real, and she'd never had a fright like that before.

She wrapped a dressing-gown around her and opened the door. The house was quiet, the passage in darkness, as she felt her way along the wall to her brother's room. She opened the door and closed it behind her, switched on the light.

Joe's room was full of aeroplane models, and she had to move carefully to avoid them. She sat on the edge of his bed and shook him hard; Joe was a heavy sleeper.

Presently, her brother stirred. 'What's up, then? Mandy . . .'

'I had a nightmare, Joe. It scared me—I've got to talk to somebody.'

Joe was twelve, two years younger than his sister, and sturdy, with unruly fair hair.

Mandy shuddered. 'It was horrid!'

Joe sat up reluctantly; he was still sleepy. 'What was it about?'

'I was walking alone, through a mist, and all round me were ruins. It was nowhere I've ever seen, I'm sure of that. And then *she* came towards me, through the mist. Her feet didn't touch the ground—she just drifted along. I could see right through her, Joe. She was a ghost, a girl of about my age in a long dress, and with a pale face. Her mouth was moving as if she was trying to say something, but I couldn't hear what it was—like watching the old silent movies on telly. That's all, really, because I woke up. But it was so real.' She forced a laugh. 'I don't know why I was scared so much—it was only a dream.'

Joe rubbed sleep from his eyes and looked hard at his sister. 'You do look a bit white . . . Still, I never heard of anyone dreaming a ghost before.' He sounded impressed.

Mandy stood up. 'I'll be all right now, Joe. Thanks for listening.'

She tiptoed back to her room, and it was a long time before she fell asleep.

A week later, Mandy dreamed again. She stood among the ruins of an old house and it was dark. The ghost girl appeared before her, rippling as if seen through water. She felt icy cold. The ghost drifted nearer and lifted an arm, reaching out a hand to touch her . . .

Mandy awoke abruptly, soaked with sweat, her heart thumping wildly. She pushed bedclothes into her mouth to stop herself screaming. It was ridiculous, she thought, scared silly by a dream . . .

At the breakfast table, her mother commented: 'You look off-colour, Mandy. Are you sleeping all right?'

Joe hastily swallowed a spoonful of cereal. 'Was it the dream again?'

Their father looked up from his newspaper crossword. 'What dream's this? First I've heard of it.'

'She dreamed a ghost,' Joe said proudly.

'A ghost?' Father looked interested. 'That's jolly original.'

Mother said, 'Well, don't do it again if it's going to make you ill.'

Mandy made a silent prayer that she would never dream that particular dream again. Ever.

Another week passed before the dream returned. This time Mandy was exploring overgrown shubbery in the large garden surrounding the ruins. And when the ghost girl reached out a hand to touch her, the ground opened and Mandy fell into darkness. She was falling, falling . . .

She woke up screaming. The bedroom door opened and the light came on. Mother came in hurriedly, looking concerned.

'What is it, Mandy?'

'The dream,' she sobbed. 'The ghost came for me again!'

Mother put her arms around her, and gradually she quietened down. 'I'll leave the light on—and in the morning I'm taking you to see Dr Thomson. We can't have this going on any longer.'

Dr Thomson was a chubby little man with a red face and bushy grey hair. After he'd listened to Mandy's story, he admitted: 'This is a new one on me. Let's see now, you break up for the holidays soon—are you going away?'

'To Devon, to stay with an uncle. That's next week.'

'Not next week,' the doctor said briskly. 'Right now. Today. There's nothing like a change of air and a bit of exercise. Perhaps you've been studying too hard.'

At home, father made a phone call while mother packed two cases. Mandy and Joe got in the car, waving goodbye to mother as they drove off.

Mandy began to feel better already as the car gathered speed on the main road to Exeter.

'It'll be fun,' Joe said. 'Uncle George and Ben and Polly. And Dartmoor to explore.'

Uncle George was an artist and designed sleeves for pop records; he was easy-going and the children could do what they liked. He was a widower and had only recently moved to a cottage on Dartmoor.

It was late afternoon when they arrived, driving across the desolate moor to a small cottage set beside a stream between hills. Pop music blared from a record-player. The children, Ben and Polly, came running out to greet them.

'Now we can have fun!' Ben shouted.

Mandy's father stayed for a meal before driving home, and Uncle George told him: 'She'll be all right here. A few days on the moor and she'll be too exhausted to dream. My two sleep like logs.'

It began to seem that Uncle George was right. In the days that followed, the four children explored the wild moor, hunting for bronze-age relics and barrows, chasing wild ponies, climbing the high tors. There was Devon cream for tea, and Mandy's skin turned nut-brown in the sun and wind; she felt fitter than she'd ever felt before—and the dream didn't come back to bother her.

Uncle George was at his easel, immersed in a new painting, and Polly and Mandy were cutting sandwiches. Ben announced: 'Today we're going to the old house for a picnic. It's a super place to play hide-and-seek.'

'OK, kids,' Uncle George said absently. 'Mind you get back before dark.'

It was a bright sunny day when they set out, walking between ferns and yellow-flowering gorse. Ben, who had short legs and was inclined to be on the tubby side, complained: 'Not so fast.'

'Oh, come on, Fatty!'

'Shut your face, Pretty Poll!'

Polly—who *was* pretty—ran ahead, blonde hair streaming. 'Can't catch me!'

The moor was empty of life except for some sheep in the distance.

'What's this old house?' Joe asked.

'It's not a house really, not any more. Just the ruins of one. But there are lots of walls standing, and thick shrubbery. No one ever goes there, so we'll have the place to ourselves.'

When they reached the ruins, all four were hungry, and Mandy and Polly set out their picnic lunch.

Mandy was finishing her sandwiches and drinking lemonade when she began to look around with fresh interest. She had the eerie feeling she knew this place; but that was impossible— she'd never been on Dartmoor before. The feeling persisted and the memory of her dream returned.

All at once she began to shiver. This was the place she'd dreamed . . .

Joe asked: 'Are you all right, Mandy?'

She nodded. 'It's just that this place reminds me of my dream. I'll get over it.' She jumped to her feet. 'Come on, let's play hide-and-seek.'

'I'll be seeker first,' Joe said.

Mandy and Ben and Polly ran off to hide while Joe shut his eyes and began to count to a hundred.

Mandy ran towards the shrubbery; it was thick and green with a lot of cover to hide in. Yet, as she approached, she felt curiously reluctant to enter the dark bushes. Behind her, Joe finished counting and called:

'Look out—I'm coming!'

Mandy took a deep breath and forced her way into the matted undergrowth. She moved slowly and quietly, and the green leaves closed above her head, shutting out the sun. She began to feel cold and lonely. She pressed deeper and deeper into the shrubbery, following what might once have been a path but was now grown over with weeds and wild flowers.

Far enough, Mandy thought—Joe won't find me here. She took a few more steps forward, and then . . .

Mist curled up from the ground in front of her and shaped itself into a human figure. Mandy stopped dead, her heart in her mouth. She was looking at the ghost girl of her dreams, a young girl wearing an old-fashioned frock. Her face was pale and her expression sad. The ghost wavered in the air before Mandy's staring eyes—and she could see dark green leaves through the wraith.

The ghost shimmered as it drifted towards her. Mandy stood paralysed, her legs turned to jelly. A slender arm was lifted and a hand reached out, touched her. The touch was as cold as ice, and it burned.

Mandy jumped. She turned and bolted in panic, crashing through the bushes till she burst out into sunshine and collapsed on the grass.

Joe raced up, calling: 'Mandy! What's the matter?'

'The ghost, Joe . . . I saw her.' She pointed to the bushes. 'In there.'

'I'm going to look,' Joe said fiercely. 'I'll settle that old ghost.' He went into the shubbery, determined, but moving warily.

Ben and Polly joined Mandy as Joe returned. He had a thoughtful expression on his face. 'I didn't see your ghost,' he said. 'What I did see was a dark, deep well. So it was lucky you did see her just then. We've got to tell Uncle George about this.'

Next day, Uncle George and a policeman visited the hidden well. At the bottom they found the skeleton of a young girl, which was later brought up and buried in the local churchyard.

How terrible, Mandy thought, to die like that.

She never dreamed of her ghost-girl again, though she tried. She would have liked the ghost to come back—just once—so she could thank the girl for saving her life. In a strange way, she knew she had lost a friend.

But Mandy never forgot her. She was reminded of her every time she looked at her wrist, at the marks that never completely faded—marks left where ghostly fingers had touched her.

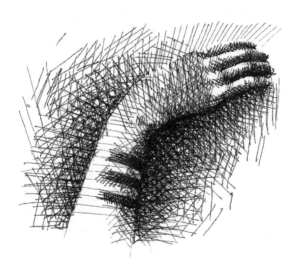

The Lost Child

JOHN BURKE

At first she tried to pretend that it was the wind. Or perhaps it was merely the uneasy whimper a child makes when turning over in its sleep. She stirred the cocoa slowly in the pan, leaning her forehead against the low mantelpiece and willing herself to hear nothing out of the ordinary. There had been no sound: it was her imagination, could be nothing else.

But she was still listening. Despite the warmth of the fire prickling in her cheeks she felt a chill down her back.

No, not again. She couldn't go through it again . . .

It was not the wind. It came, faint and unmistakable, from the room above.

Mrs Neal took the pan away from the fire and waited for her knees to stop trembling. The cry might be an ordinary one—fear of the dark, wanting a drink, or just calling out for the sake of calling out—and then she would have only to utter a few reassuring words. She would watch with pleasure Janet's sleepy smile, always so elusive and fascinating when the light of the candle chased it into the shadows at the corner of her mouth. And for a moment there would be the drowsiness of Janet's voice. The kitchen was always too quiet after Janet had gone to bed; the silence was like a curtain draped about the room, with no one to disturb its thick, oppressive folds.

Once there had been Hugh, his legs stretched out towards the fire, his lazy voice chasing away the mists of loneliness that seemed to creep out of the very walls of this cottage, standing solitary upon its bleak hillside. Once there had been Hugh; but no more. Hugh would not have been frightened by a little girl's dream. Hugh would have gone upstairs without hesitation instead of fingering the handle of the pan and pretending that it might not be necessary after all to light the candle and go up the creaking stairs.

For a third time she heard the cry.

She took the oil lamp from the table. On each of the past three evenings she had taken the candle so that its flickering light would not glare into Janet's eyes. But tonight she was scared. Tonight she would carry the defiant brightness of the lamp into that bedroom.

The wind from the moors whispered along the hillside and in through the ill-fitting back door, chasing her with mocking gusts up the stairs.

Janet's voice was clear now.

'Mummy, where are you? Come a bit nearer, please.'

Mrs Neal opened the door.

Tonight the feeling of enmity was stronger. It was something tangible, lurking beyond the radiance of the lamp. It jeered at her as she set the lamp down on the dressing-table beside the photograph of Hugh in uniform. He smiled out at her but was incapable of offering any reassurance.

Janet dragged her arms out from under the sheet.

'Mummy, it's coming again. Stop it, or I'll be lost again. Lost . . . Don't let it, Mummy.'

Her eyelids were closed but trembling. Just as they had been on Christmas Eve when she was pretending to sleep, thought her mother. The happy comparison was incongruous: in this bedroom now there was nothing but terror.

'I'm here, Janet,' she said quietly. She sat on the edge of the bed and took hold of one of the clutching, aimless hands.

'Mummy, it's here again. It wants me. It's after me. Stop it—do something before it's too late and I've slipped away again. Oh, *please* . . .'

The appeal ended in a whimper of anguish.

Mrs Neal said: 'Janet, darling, I'm here.'

The hand freed itself from her grasp and waved her away. She seized it again as though she herself needed support.

'Jan—'

The child frowned and muttered. 'It's no good, Mummy. It's still too strong. I'm going . . . going. But I'll be back soon. When you call me loud enough. You must make it very loud. I can't hold on now.'

'You're all right,' said the woman desperately. She was sobbing in the back of her throat because she did not know what she was fighting or why she had to fight. 'You're not going anywhere, Jan. You're with me. You're safe.'

'Going . . .'

Janet's eyes opened. The lamp glittered in them so that at first it looked as though she had been blinded by tears. Then the film was wiped away. Her mouth twisted in the slight smile that was so breathtakingly like Hugh's smile.

She said: 'Hello, Mummy.'

Mrs Neal drew a deep breath. She had got her daughter back. They had been separated and were reunited. It was the fourth time.

The fourth time. This would have to be stopped somehow.

She must tread warily so that Janet would not be frightened. 'Jan, darling . . .' But how to begin?

'Talking in my sleep again?' said Janet in a small voice.

'Yes, you certainly were.' She forced a laugh and tried to sound casual. 'What were you dreaming about this time?'

Her daughter turned her dark head on the pillow and stared at the wall. She began to trace wavering outlines in the air with one finger. 'The same as last night, I think. And other nights, too. But I'm not sure. I jus' think so, that's all.'

'Not many people dream the same dream four nights running.'

'Don't they?'

'What a queer little girl you are, aren't you?'

'I don't know.'

'You were talking about going away. Who were you going away from? Or can't you remember?' Fear leapt from the shadows beyond the lamp like a sly cat.

'Can't 'member much. But I was leaving Mummy. I was being pulled away from my mummy.'

'Well, it didn't come true, did it? I'm here, and you're still here.'

Janet rolled over on her back. She looked puzzled. 'That's right.' But she was doubtful. 'You're here and I'm here. But . . .' She could find no words.

'Well,' said her mother briskly, 'you've no business to be awake and talking at this time of night, anyway. I'll tuck you up again and then we'll have some sleep, shall we—without any dreams.'

Without any dreams. She prayed for that on the way downstairs. She could not conceive what would happen if this went on. Each time it was becoming harder to recall Janet from the strange world into which she had wandered: in four nights she seemed to have penetrated deeper and deeper into it, getting further away from any voice that tried to call her back. Mrs Neal felt there would come a time—perhaps soon, too soon— when the two of them would lose touch with each other altogether. She was in a dream herself, a dream in which she ran without moving and reached out with her arms towards an eight-year-old girl who grew smaller and smaller as she was dragged into the distance.

At breakfast next morning she waited for Janet to say something. Janet, however, finished her milk without mentioning the dreams. It was not until the end of the meal that, as though recalling something which perplexed her, she looked about the small room with a questioning tilt of her head and asked suddenly:

'This *is* home, isn't it?'

'Of course it is, chick.'

'I was just wondering. I thought there was something funny.' Then she seemed to accept everything as abruptly as she had questioned it, and there was nothing unusual in her expression as she grinned across the table. 'I'd better hurry, hadn't I?'

Mrs Neal made her decision. It was a decision she had contemplated in the middle of the night as she lay awake and from which she had backed away in the cold, welcome light of morning. She returned to it now because in one blinding second she had visualized what it would be like when evening came again, when the curtains were drawn and she stood by the fire making supper, or sat reading and sewing, not daring to switch on the harsh old radio in the corner in case its tinny voice drowned the noise she dreaded to hear but could not ignore. Not another evening like that; no more evenings like that!

She said: 'You're not going to school this morning. We're going to see the doctor.'

'Why? What do I have to go to the doctor's for? I don't feel poorly.'

'I'm sure there's something wrong with . . . with your inside. All those funny dreams. It must be bad digestion or something.'

'But I don't have a tummy-ache.'

'I've had enough of running upstairs and lying awake,' said her mother crisply, 'wondering if you're going to call out.'

Janet said: 'I'm all right, really. I mean, I don't *mind* the dreams.'

'Don't mind them? But you're always struggling and thrashing about, and crying about going away and leaving me.'

'I don't think so. Not really, Mummy. I can't tell you all about them because I can't remember now, but I know they're awfully nice in parts. A nice sort of place, and lovely people, and . . . and . . .'

'What about the going-away part?' She clenched her fists below the table because she had said such a dangerous, provocative thing.

Janet looked down into her empty mug and swung it round as though swilling milk about at the bottom. 'Going away? Mm . . . I think that's what comes at the end. It's not the dreams I mind. It's when I'm leaving the place and . . .' She looked quickly at her mother, surprised and unsure of herself; and then looked away.

Leaving the place, thought Mrs Neal. And waking up. Was it leaving the land of her dream and being forced to wake up, or being unable to stay asleep any longer, that made Janet cry out in protest?

Her mouth was dry with fright. 'But where do I come in?' she persisted. 'It's me that you're afraid of leaving, isn't it? It's me that you call out to in your dream.'

'Do I?' Janet looked unnaturally cunning, quite unlike her usual self. 'I don't know. At least . . . I seem to remember being pulled away from my mummy. But . . .' She stopped. There was something in her mind which she would not let herself say. Abruptly she asked: 'Mummy, how do you know which is which?'

'How do you mean, dear?'

'Which is dreams and which is . . . the real thing?'

Then her features puckered up and she began to cry.

Full of remorse, Mrs Neal got up and went to put her arms round her daughter. She was surprised at the quiet resistance Janet offered.

They walked together to the village in an inexplicably hostile silence. The threatening grey sky weighed down heavily upon them.

Dr Scott shook his head.

'I don't claim to be a witch doctor. There are times when I like some assistance in making my diagnosis. What am I supposed to be looking for, Mary? I can't find anything wrong.'

Mrs Neal glanced at Janet.

The doctor said: 'Just sit in the room with the magazines, will you, Janet? We won't keep you waiting long.'

When the two of them were alone together he waited for Mrs Neal to speak. It took her a few fumbling moments to get anything out.

'I don't know what to say. I mean—oh dear, Philip, I've forced myself to come here and get it all off my chest, and now I'm sure it'll sound a lot of nonsense.'

'Most of my patients trot out the most marvellous varieties of nonsense without feeling the slightest shame. Just reel off the symptoms and I'll trot out my answers.'

Symptoms? She told him as best she could, stumbling over this explanation of the inexplicable. When she had finished she wished she could have retracted every word. Overwhelmingly conscious that it was now broad daylight, she began to stammer out excuses and qualifications.

Dr Scott shook his head brusquely. 'Don't try to back out now, Mary. You believed in what you were saying while you were saying it. There must be a reason for that. And if you think, now you've listened to your own story, that it sounds silly, there must be a reason for that, too. You're afraid, aren't you?'

'For Janet.'

'Are you sure of that? You feel that this is something more than a physical matter—something more than just a tummy-ache. But is it really Janet who's suffering: is Janet the patient, or . . .?'

'I don't follow.'

'Let's be honest about it. You can be frank with me, Mary. Even more important, I want you to be frank with yourself. Are you sure'—he was speaking with great deliberation—'that this nightmare, if it *is* a nightmare so far as Janet's concerned, is in itself worrying you? Are you sure it's not a little something in your subconscious which has been stirred up, so that you're reading things into the dream that aren't there?'

'I don't follow,' she said again.

'Perhaps you're too conscientious. You're too keyed-up about every little detail. I know what a struggle you've had and how lonely you've been.'

'Not lonely,' she said quickly; 'not with Janet there.'

'Aren't you perhaps asking too much of Janet? She's everything to you. I've no doubt you reproach yourself for every little thing that goes wrong with her, however insignificant. And when she dreams, you feel that her dreams show some sort of psychological dissatisfaction with *you*.'

'No. No, I don't think so. I don't look at things in that way. At least, I don't think I do.'

'You're too serious, Mary. You take things too earnestly.' She felt hopelessly that it was no good stopping him, no good telling him that he was on the wrong track altogether. 'In the first place,' he said brightly, 'is Janet frightened by these dreams?'

'She calls out for me as she's waking up.'

'But the dreams themselves—does she remember them in detail? Does she say they're horrible?'

'No,' Mrs Neal reluctantly admitted. 'She . . . she says they're quite nice.'

His gentle look of triumph was intolerable. So was his equally gentle offer to arrange for her to see a nerve specialist if she wished. And in the meantime, a tonic. Perhaps something soothing that would stop her worrying, until she herself came to accept that everything was all right.

She left him in a mood of rejection, as though she had been deserted by the only friend on whom she had relied. Janet walked silently beside her as they left the village and went back up the hill towards the forlorn little cottage, its bedroom windows like eyes watching them as they approached.

The doctor's voice rang in her head. Subconscious guilt about something—something absurd, as he had cheerfully assured her. You haven't neglected the child. You worry too much. The loss of her father wasn't your fault, you've done your best to fill his place, there's nothing with which to reproach yourself. Symbolism . . . child losing mother . . . insufficiency, guilt, pessimism . . . it's all in *your* mind, not in hers.

Just a recurrent dream—unusual, but nothing more.

And when, right at the end, suddenly bursting out with her fear, she had said, 'Do you believe in possession—in being possessed by . . . other forces?' he had risen from his chair and spoken to her gravely, an old friend concerned for her welfare, talking once more about nerve specialists and tonics and sedatives.

It was useless. How could she hope to convince him that it was not a prescription for a bottle of coloured liquid that she needed? While she repeated to herself the terrifying word 'possession' he talked about slight mental disturbances, strange fantasies. Unpleasant ideas, to be sure; but she would have been almost glad to believe him. When darkness crept down the hill and up from the village, encompassing the house, she would not have been frightened if only she could have attached a neat little clinical label to it all. A matter of psychology: it was a concept to drive out night fears, a comforting explanation of anything that made you uneasy. You could use it as a sort of magic charm, brandishing it in the face of monsters, spirits, phantoms. Anything would crumple and scuttle away before that cold, beautiful word.

If you believed in it.

When the first cry came that night, she sat down and picked up the book she had been reading, concentrating on the page at which it had lain open for a good fifteen minutes. No need to go upstairs. Janet was dreaming, but dreams could do no harm. It was better to stay downstairs. She herself was the only one who could suffer from hearing what went on in Janet's dreams. Symbolism, subconscious . . . she tried over the lovely musical syllables and tried to assure herself that they made everything all right.

She remained seated for a full ten minutes and then put the book down because the print was tilting at absurd angles across the page and the sentences did not make sense and the lamplight did not seem as bright as it had been. She turned up the wick and carried the lamp upstairs.

Janet's quiet plaintive voice increased in volume as the door opened, like a radio sharply turned up.

'And down there by the pool . . . Mummy, are we really together now? I'm sorry about last night, but I didn't know. Truly I didn't. I thought that was real. If it goes and happens again . . . but you won't let it, will you? You won't? But if it *did* happen again, I'd hold on tight like you said, and I'd still be me instead of being . . . whatever it was.'

Mrs Neal lowered herself warily on to the edge of the bed. Janet uneasily turned her closed eyes towards the light.

'It's coming,' she moaned.

'I'm here, Jan. Wake up.'

She wanted to seize Janet by the shoulders and shake her into wakefulness, but was afraid. She was scared to do more than speak slowly and clearly, hoping her voice would penetrate to that country beyond sleep where Janet was pausing indecisively.

'I'm here, Jan. You're all right. You're at home, you're safe. I'm not going away.'

'Mummy, it's come again. Hold me. I promise not to let go this time. And you won't let me, will you?'

'You're safe. No one's going to take you away.'

Janet twisted and burrowed into the pillow as though to prevent herself waking up. The things she muttered were lost, but there was no mistaking the note of urgency. Mrs Neal began to sob. She longed even more to reach out and shake her little girl. Surely it would be best done now, before it was too late?

But she went on talking, not altogether sure of what she was saying.

'Janet, wake up, darling. Come along, now—I won't let you slip away.'

'It's coming,' said Janet tensely. 'But this time it'll be all right. I know it'll be all right. You promise, don't you? Promise. I'm me, and I'm staying me. I'll be back soon. Back right away.'

She turned again, her eyelids fluttering as she screwed them up against the light.

'Jan . . .'

Janet's eyes opened. There was the same film that had been there before, then it slipped away. Janet was awake.

Mrs Neal was trembling with the effort of expending all her forces in that mental strain, reaching into the unknown for her daughter. She let out a sigh now, and waited for the familiar smile. It was over. Janet was back and now she would smile.

But there was no smile. No recognition. The hard, childishly honest eyes stared at her and the mouth twitched slightly. Janet said:

'Who are you?'

'Janet, wake up. The dream's all over and you're home. In bed. It's all over, darling.'

'Who are you?' repeated the child, drawing back.

Mrs Neal gulped down the terror rising in her throat. She said desperately: 'You're home, Janet. Jan, don't look at me like that. You're all right now.'

'No. I'm lost now.' The girl let out a sudden cry of anguish. 'I'm lost. But I'm still me. I must remember that. This is the nightmare my mummy told me about. This is it. But it'll be all right.'

'Janet, darling—'

'This is a nightmare,' said the child as though repeating a lesson. 'Soon I'll wake up again. Mummy said I would.'

Mrs Neal reached out. But it was too late now. She knew it was too late. The little girl's eyes were wide open and she was cowering away, shaking her head in fear.

'Leave me alone. Don't touch me.' The lamp threw great shadows under her eyes. 'Who are you?' She looked wildly about the room and recognized nothing. 'When will I wake up?' she cried. 'Oh, when will I wake up?'

The Gargles

MICHAEL CHISLETT

They are up there! Look! See the gargles.'

Tish put on her glasses to look at where Sam, her five-year-old brother, pointed up through the fine rain to see what was on the library roof.

'Gargoyles, Sam,' she corrected. The word was difficult for him to pronounce. 'I've never noticed them before. Do they come alive and swoop down on people?'

'No, that's terrydactiles do that. They climb down, then chase after you.'

The building stood between the town hall and theatre on the Broadway. Tish wondered why she had never seen them, never been told about them until now. But then her eyes were so weak that unless she wore the ugly spectacles with their thick lenses she could not see very much at all.

They peered over and down from the roof, Gothic monsters

in the heart of suburban London. The thought of the creatures watching and not being seen by her disturbed Tish, who imagined them creeping down the walls like lizards to the pavement where they would lift their muzzles to sniff the air for prey, slinking between the market stalls on the Broadway and through the shopping centre then into the car park beneath the flats where they could stalk a victim through that cavernous place as it rang with the clash of shopping trolleys, passing as dogs or shadows on murky December afternoons such as this one, not recognized for what they really were until too late.

Sam pulled urgently on her hand. 'Come on, Tish, I want to go home.'

It might have been the drizzle blurring her glasses but Tish was sure that one of the things leant further out over the roof to survey the world below.

After walking but a few paces Sam came to an abrupt stop before a toy stall. As he gazed with longing at its wares Tish looked up at the roof. A pair of the monsters stood together, clawed hands gripping the roof's edge, deep in conversation about something, or someone. She was positive that they had not been there a moment before.

A cloud of misty rain concealed them as Sam took off on his precipitate way again with Tish in tow. Forcibly she stopped him and removed the spectacles, not wanting anyone to see her wearing the things. Miserably she thought of how her eyesight seemed to be getting worse. The doctor had warned her that she must wear them all the time to stop this, but she just could not, they were so awful, making her look bug-eyed and hideous.

As they walked hand in hand through the shopping centre Tish thought it odd that she had lived all her life just minutes away from them yet the gargoyles had never come to her attention. Perhaps they hadn't wanted to be seen by her until now?

'Race you, Tish!' Sam challenged after they had crossed the road from the car park, and without waiting for her he ran off laughing as she trailed behind.

Tish didn't feel like running, she didn't feel very well at all, which was why she hadn't gone to school.

'Do you have to bash on the door like that?' their mother said crossly. 'Why aren't you wearing your glasses?'

'It was Sam who knocked, not me,' Tish said and put on the spectacles. 'If I wear them in the rain they get all smudgy so there's no point. Did you know that there are gargoyles on the library roof, Mum? Sam told me. I never knew they were there.'

With an indifferent shrug her mother wandered back to the television, her usual reaction to most things told to her. It seemed to Tish that all her mother ever did was complain about her growing so tall and needing new clothes, and not wearing those horrid spectacles. Sighing, she looked out of the rain-smeared window. The afternoon was so dismal and it would soon be full dark. Tish wished that she had gone to school, wished that she hadn't felt ill that morning, wished for so many things.

Tish and Sam played in the bedroom, building up plastic bricks that he instantly knocked down. Tiring of this she crawled across the floor, her face contorted into an evil grimace, saying, 'I am a gargle and I'm going to get you, Sam, and massacre you all up.'

'Don't Tish,' he cried in alarm. 'I don't like them, they frighten me.'

'I'll protect you from them,' Tish promised and hugged her brother. 'They don't really come alive.'

'They do, they watch all the time,' Sam insisted.

'I wish that you would stop scaring him.' Their mother glared in the doorway.

'I'm not scaring him,' Tish argued, 'just playing. Sam knows that, don't you?'

'Clear this mess up and come down, your dinner's ready.'

'You won't let them get me, will you, Tish?' Sam asked nervously.

'Of course not, they're not real.' She hugged him again. 'Let's tidy up and I'll tell you a real good story before I go out.'

'And just as the gargle was going to pounce on her she pulled out the mirror hidden beneath her coat and the monster looked at it and stopped, looked at it again and screamed. The gargle was so ugly and had never looked in a mirror in its life, never seen itself, and the sight was so horrible that it turned back to stone right there from shock. So she took out a hammer and smashed the old gargle into a zillion pieces and the Dauntless

Girl released all the witches that the monster had captured.'

'That was a good one, Tish,' said Sam. 'What did she look like, that girl? What was her name, and what's "dauntless"?'

'She was tall and slim with brown hair and "dauntless" means that she didn't have any daunts on her. It just means that she was brave. Don't know her name. How about oh . . . Olive? She wore glasses too, clever people all do.'

'It's you then,' Sam grinned. 'You've got brown hair and you're tall and skinny and you're brave. You were when you had that operation on your eyes, the doctor said you was. Don't go out, Tish. Stay in and tell me another story about you.'

'I have to meet Donna,' she said and checked her watch. Sam was so restless, not wanting to go to sleep. Tish knew that her mother would complain if she left him like that. But if she didn't hurry, then she would be late. Why her mother could not put Sam to bed just once, or even let him stay up a little later, she didn't know. No one, not even a five year old, went to bed at this time.

'Be careful', he warned as Tish kissed him goodnight, 'of them gargles.'

'I'm going out now', she told her mother, 'to meet Donna.'

'Funny how you was too ill to go to school this morning but are all right now to go out. Don't be late again. I want you in by eleven.'

'Thirty,' said Tish. 'See you later.'

The drizzle hadn't stopped and even if she hadn't taken the glasses off as soon as she stepped out of the door Tish would hardly have been able to see clearly. The world was more blurred and indistinct than ever. The orange glow of the street lights floated like goldfish in the misty air. She walked down a drowned street, in a watery world.

Tish had not been quite truthful about who she was going to see. Ricky had promised to meet her at eight and it was five past now. Anxious to save time she ran through the car park, feet echoing in the deserted cavern until on reaching the shopping centre she slowed to a rapid walk. It was good to have long legs for some things.

Ricky was not there where they were supposed to meet on the opposite side of the Broadway. He was late again. Standing in a shop doorway out of the rain Tish watched neon lights flash on and off by the theatre, vividly lighting the night for brief seconds to advertise a Christmas show. As they shone the roof of the adjacent library was revealed for an instant and she put on her glasses to look up there.

They were there, in the night and misty rain, revealed for a moment by a lightning flash of neon, then taken by the darkness again. Watching back at her. She would tell Ricky when he arrived. She had to see him, and he had promised to come. It was half past now. Had she said half past instead of eight?

Tish took off the glasses and her eyes blurred over as she waited. The whole world turned to water about her as she sank deeper into the flood.

It was after eleven when Tish got off the bus at the Broadway. She had waited for an hour but he had not come, could not be bothered. She felt a fool for waiting in the cold and wet. Rather than go back home she had boarded a bus and ridden it to the end of the route, then travelled back on it, nursing her hurt and anger.

The neon lights had been switched off but she still looked up at the roof to see nothing but mist and dark. Tish imagined the gargles might have climbed down and got Ricky. It would be nice to be a witch and make them do things like that. She imagined the things, composed of the nastier parts of lizard and canine, pursuing him. The thought was curiously satisfying. But then they could be chasing after her.

Tish walked as far away from the building as possible, but still it encroached on her dim vision. The once familiar place now seemed monstrous to her, the home of devils, nightmares, and night-daunts.

Seeing a movement in the shopping centre through which she was about to walk Tish stopped. Something crouched by a rubbish bin. Was it a dog at its contents? Hard to be sure for everything was blurred worse than usual, for, though she hated to admit it, Tish had cried quite a lot. She had discovered the real reason why her eyes were like they were. They were full of tears that had to be all cried out before she would ever be able to see properly.

She decided to take the long way home, down the turning by the railway which would lead to her own street. A bit longer but she did not now care to go through the shopping centre and car park.

The side street was dark after the relative brightness of the Broadway. The trees and bushes by the railway gave that part of the road a wild, dangerous look—just the place to hide on a night obscured all the more by misty rain. Shivering, Tish wondered why she had gone that way.

'I like to live on the edge,' she muttered, her breath becoming one with the mist and rain. 'I'm that sort of girl. Shame that I can't see the edge without those glasses on. If anything did happen to me tonight would Ricky feel guilty?'

Sharp and sudden the sound came from the railway line. Something moved on top of the wall there, moved swiftly in the light from the track. It could be a fox, there were lots of them about. If only she had seen it clearly.

Hearing another scratching, scuttling noise behind her as she turned the corner, Tish ran the last few yards home until at her door she looked down the street. She could see nothing for the drizzle in her eyes.

A heart-shrivelling wail greeted her as she entered and Tish looked into the front room to see that Sam lay on the settee, his face pale and damp with sweat as he held his arms out to her.

'What's the matter with him?' she asked her mother.

'He's been having nightmares, that's what,' she answered angrily. 'Look at the time. You're late! I can't get him to sleep because you've been telling him stories and frightening him. You and the silly tales you make up!'

'I haven't been telling him any stories,' Tish retorted. 'Not bad ones anyway.'

Sam's cry distracted Tish from confrontation and she made

soothing noises to him as he rocked his head from side to side in agitation.

'I'm here now, Sammy, your big sister's here to look after you.'

'Take him back to bed,' her mother snapped. 'I've missed half my programme now!'

'They was looking in the window, Tish,' Sam told her as she put him to bed. 'I was frightened of them gargles because they was looking for you. Come to bed with me, Tish.' He was mumbling, half-asleep already.

'Just for a minute. I'll give you a cuddle.' She took off her wet coat and shoes then her jeans and climbed in with him. 'Don't be frightened of dreams, Sam, they can't hurt you. Who was it told you that they was there on the library roof?'

'Called me and I saw 'em, not a dream. Don't want them gargles taking you, Tish.'

'They're not real things, Sam, just statues.'

He placed his arm protectively over her and they lay silent until Sam began to snore gently and this sound soothed Tish so much that she too fell asleep.

Stone against stone, claws scraping on the roof. The sound woke Tish out of a dream in which she stood on a high place and looked down at the world, her sight sharp and clear, able to see everything, the edge that was so near and dangerous. She listened but the noise had stopped. Sam's sigh was the only break in the silence as he held her close. As gently as possible she moved his arm off her and climbed from the bed, shivering at the sudden cold. The clock's illuminated dial read two o'clock and a groan passed through the house as if some great weight shifted on it.

After wriggling into her jeans and putting on her glasses Tish peeped through the curtains and saw that the sky was clearing and the moon and stars showed through scraps of ragged cloud. Then one by one, down the length of the street, the lamps were extinguished, blown out like the lights on a birthday cake to plunge the world outside into blackness. She felt panic as night and dark conspired to close in on her.

Was this what it would be like if she did go blind?

Seeing the lights of London glowing faintly in the distance Tish realized that it could only be a power cut, nothing to be frightened of. She crept out of the bedroom, a raging thirst in her throat. She would try the lights downstairs, get a drink, then go to her own bed.

To her relief the kitchen light worked. She poured a glassful of milk and saw her face reflected in the window, the great insect-eyes. A double reflection, for something stood behind her, so Tish pulled the curtain shut, not wanting to see herself or whatever else might be there. In the night, with her dim eyes, everything seen in a glass was seen darkly. It was so hard to tell what one looked at or what looked back at you.

She sat for a while in the front room, thinking. The curtains at the window had been drawn but they stirred ever so slightly in a draught. The window might be open just a fraction and if it was it would be easy for someone to open it from the outside. She should check, but the thought of what might look out of the night at her was unnerving. If she made no sound, did not show herself, then she would be safe. To do something stupid, like opening a door, or even a curtain, would be an invitation. It was best not to encourage the powers of darkness for, she realized, this would be admitting their existence and once that was done you might be theirs forever.

The door swung abruptly open and Tish jumped up, her arms out to ward them off.

'I woke up and you wasn't there,' Sam sobbed, 'but they were and wanted you.'

'Oh, Sam! It's only dreams, nightmares, nothing's there really.' The curtains stirred again. 'There's nothing to be frightened of, not when I'm with you.'

'Make Nothing go away,' he demanded, 'like you did in your story.'

'Nothing's not anyone or anything, not a name, Sam. You only dreamed things. Let's go back to bed and I'll show you.'

But as she spoke these words the thought nagged. What if they are there? What if they are looking for me? Might they take Sammy and hurt him?

The sound of footsteps on the stairs made Tish freeze. They were coming down for her and she had nowhere to hide. Why come to her? What had she done?

A cry shuddered through the house and Tish and Sam answered it in sympathy as they held each other tightly and a voice came from outside, at the door. 'Open the door and let me in.' The voice sounded like their mother's, but not quite. 'I've hurt myself and can't manage it.'

'What have you done?' Tish asked suspiciously.

Groans and creaks filled the house as strange things stirred and woke.

'Broken something. Now let me in.'

'What have you broken?'

'My heart. You broke it for me. Now open the door right now, Patricia. If you don't do it this instant I shall be really cross with you.'

Tish stared at the door. Her mother never called her Patricia, nobody did.

'I know where you have been tonight.' The voice had changed, not her mother's at all now. 'I saw you waiting for that boy. You started to cry when he didn't come. He was with another girl and who can blame him. A girl who doesn't have to wear thick ugly goggles to see where she's going. A girl who's not taller than he is. A girl who's not as skinny as you. Olive Oil they call you. What a nickname!'

'Go away,' Tish said as angry tears filled her eyes. 'Leave us alone.'

'If you don't open the door then we will have to open it and we'll get you anyway and we will hurt Sammy and you will get the blame.'

'Don't let Nothing hurt me, Tish,' Sam pleaded. 'I'm frightened.'

There was a scratch at the window like a cat asking to be let in and another voice spoke from outside. 'We'll take little Sam away up onto the roof where we will do things with him and to him. He won't like these things.'

'It's them gargles,' Sam whispered. 'Stop 'em, Tish, don't let them have me.'

'We will have you, Sam, oh yes, if we can't have your goggle-eyed sister.'

'I haven't done anything to deserve it, nothing to be taken away for!' Tish cried.

'Haven't you!' the voices exclaimed together. 'Are you sure, Olive Oil? Something that you are going to have to tell your mum about? Something that you were going to tell Ricky about? He guessed it and that's why he didn't come.'

Tish held Sam to her. He was crying, his tears wetting her jeans. Nausea rose from her stomach and all she wanted to do was retch, spew up what was inside her. 'That's nothing to do with you!' Tears filled her eyes and she was underwater again, drowning.

Through her tears Tish looked down at Sam as he held her. She had always cared for him. Nobody else would. If there was another even more helpless, could she still mother him? But who would love and cherish her? No one at all. It would be so easy to open the door and go to whatever was there. They spoke again, not threats, but promises, seductive and gentle pleading. They really wanted her to go with them. Ricky had not. She was as ugly as a gargoyle. Her mum did not want her except to look after Sam and he wouldn't want her when he had grown a little older.

She laid him on the couch. He cried but Tish was firm and put her fingers to his lips to let him know to be quiet. She looked at herself in the mirror, the tears in her eyes gleaming like diamonds behind the thick glass of the spectacles, and ran fingers through her hair, tangled and unruly after sleep. Fourteen and five foot nine, still growing too. She would be in the school netball team if she could only see the ball.

'Too tall for my height, that's me, Olive Oil. But at least I get noticed.'

Tish decided not to take the glasses off before opening the door. It was best to see clearly what was there. No point in hiding from it. Abruptly, so as not to change her mind, she swung it open and looked out into the dark, heart beating wildly as she challenged whatever was there. Were Dauntless Girls as frightened as she was? But there was nothing, the passage was empty as was the street and when she drew the curtains to look, only her reflection stared back at her.

'Come and see, Sam,' she said. 'They've gone. I've sent them away and they won't bother us again.'

Reluctantly he came to the window to look, taking her hand, frightened that he might still be snatched away.

'You've scared them old gargles off,' he said admiringly after reassuring himself that they had really gone. 'You're that girl in your story, ain't you, Tish, that brave girl? I knew it was you.'

'I'm not really brave, Sam, it's just that my face is enough to frighten anything. I think that we had better go back to bed now.'

Tish took him up and he was soon asleep with her beside him, awake and thinking of what she must do. It was hard to be brave but she must try.

'I had nightmares last night, Tish,' Sam told her as soon as he woke. 'Them gargles was after us but you sent them away so they won't come back no more. They ought to do a story about you in a book, a comic.'

'I'm bold, I'm bold, but not too bold. I found out their names and they didn't like that. Guess what they were?'

'Dunno,' he said, 'tell us.'

'Nothing There and Nothing To Be Afraid Of. If they do come back we'll massacre the lot of 'em.'

After getting Sam up and washed and dressed, after making his breakfast, Tish went out to do her mother's shopping. She stood opposite the library looking at the roof through the thick spectacles.

How could she have mistaken them for anything but carvings, inanimate things of stone, taking life through misty rain, fear, and imagination. Nothing that could harm her or Sam at all now that she could see them clearly for what they were.

Her mother sat before the television. Tish decided to spoil that for her as well, so switched the set off. Signs of life, she thought, as her mother began to protest.

'Sit down, Mum,' said Dauntless Tish. 'I've got something to tell you.'

Blood Will Cry Out

J. J. CURLE

They say that blood will cry out from the ground for vengeance. As a solicitor I consider such ways of putting things excessive. On the other hand I freely admit the existence of coincidence. Yet was it coincidence that made me finish the letter at exactly five minutes past twelve or did Bob Stephens's blood—?

But I had better go back a little, about twelve hours to be more precise, if I am to make myself clear.

At a quarter to twelve last night I arrived home, after being out all day, to receive something of a shock. Exactly a week had passed since I had read in the *Daily Telegraph* the announcement of Bob Stephens's death, yet there in my letterbox was a letter addressed to me in what was indubitably his handwriting.

Opening it I found that it bore a date three days before the occurrence of his death!

It was a long letter, but I give it here word for word for reasons which I think you will understand when you have read it. It was for one of these reasons that I telephoned the Stephenses' house the moment I had finished it. The time when I did so, as I mentioned before, was exactly five minutes past twelve.

Dear Henry—the letter began—

I'm writing to you because there is not much time to put something right that I now realize is wrong. You probably guessed long ago about Marion and I. Well, a year ago—and I'm afraid this is going to make unpleasant reading—I made a new will.

I couldn't face you, Henry. I knew you'd never liked Marion. You always said she'd married me for money, and a year ago that was the way I saw it too. So I went to another lawyer and fixed everything without a soul that mattered knowing about it. Marion wasn't to starve, but the bulk of the money was to go to my married brother; not that he needed it, still I wanted it to stay in the family.

Now something has happened that has made me change my mind. What matters is this; the job has to be done quickly and I want *you* to do it. Marion must get the money. You're my best friend, Henry, and I think that in spite of your undemonstrative way you know it. I can trust you to see that there's no hitch even if the will's disputed—and it may be disputed. It's certainly going to look odd. I'm no lawyer but I can see that.

Now I know you, Henry, and I can just imagine you saying to yourself in that precise legal way of yours, 'Bob Stephens has always been in too much of a hurry. He married Marion in a hurry; he sold those Industrials in a hurry; and he's regretted doing both ever since. As his friend as well as his lawyer isn't it my duty to delay a little—to give him the chance to avoid a third mistake?'

Well, it won't do, Henry. That's why I've got to tell you what happened. Don't ask me to explain it. I can't. I can only give you the facts, but they're facts that add up to a cast-iron proof that I need a will drawn up as quick as you can get here to do it.

I want you here personally. I want the thing done under your eye and tied with every knot the law can devise for it. I'm morally certain you'll do what I ask, but to make doubly sure I want you to ring me *as soon as you've finished reading this letter*, no matter at what hour that may be. We can arrange then about trains. But don't forget, ring at once—any delay may be fatal.

Now for the facts, and I've got to tell them my way. Don't skip ahead. It's essential that you see them as I did to understand.

It began when I woke up last night. I don't often wake in the night and it surprised me. But over and above that I knew at once that there was something wrong. If you've ever had a blackout you'll understand what I mean. You come to in a world that seems to go right on from where it left off, and then you realize that you're in a totally different place or on your back instead of on your feet. An earthquake can be the same; they whip the world from under your feet and put it back again, but you're never quite sure if you've got the same world you started with. Well, imagine that happening but with nothing to show for it. I didn't just feel, I *knew* it had happened.

It terrified me and yet it was curiously interesting.

I got up. I had no idea what the time was, but it was pitch dark. Married men get the knack of undressing in the dark, so now I never put on a light if I've to slip across the landing at night. It was cold standing there in my room and by the time I'd decided it must be all due to a bad dream and that I might as well get back into bed, I reckoned I'd be the better for that little trip. I reached for my dressing gown on the chair and shoved a foot under the bed to feel for my slippers.

Both times I drew blank.

Now sometimes I leave them out and sometimes I put them away in the wardrobe and it's one of those things about which I'm apt to be vague, so I went over to the wardrobe and, sure enough, there they were. But what bothered me was that, for the life of me, even when I knew where they were, I couldn't remember putting them back. Anyway I got them on and opened the door.

That was when I got my second surprise. There was someone on the landing.

I couldn't see who it was, but I could hear the boards creaking and then the slur of feet on the carpet. For a moment I saw a body silhouetted against the faint light of a window and at once I realized that it was Marion. But it was not Marion as I normally knew her. There was something stilted about the way she walked that was vaguely disturbing. It was as though she was on her way to meet someone.

I expected her to go past me, for I must have been almost invisible in the doorway, but she walked right up to me and stopped. I knew she was facing me from the sound of her voice when she spoke.

Henry, that voice! There was something about this meeting in the dark, this slow ceremonial pacing, unnatural in its calmness, that had made me shiver. But hearing that voice I realized that my terror *was as nothing to Marion's.* In her voice there remained absolutely no shred of personality. It was a sound controlled with inhuman ferocity of purpose, only just on the near side of blind panic; the voice of someone accepting a death sentence.

And she was speaking to me, but somehow as though I were not there.

'What do you want, Henry?' she asked.

'I can't sleep,' I answered.

She seemed unable to reply, as though fighting for breath, and as I stood there waiting for her to go on I became aware of a most extraordinary sensation—some part of my mind seemed to penetrate hers. I could feel the blood pounding in my head as though I were suffocating. A confused redness danced before my eyes so that I thought I was going to faint. Yet at the same time I knew quite clearly that it was not I but *Marion* who was suffering these things.

As she asked the next question an impression of terrible intensity emanated from her. As far as she was concerned this was obviously the crucial moment, yet her words themselves sounded just as flat as before.

'Do you know what has happened?' she said. 'Do you remember anything?'

'Nothing's happened,' I said, my only desire now to reassure her; 'nothing's happened: I simply couldn't sleep. Now you'd better go back to your room.'

I leant towards her to take her arm and turn her in the right direction, for in her terror she seemed as unable to move as a rabbit confronted by a stoat. But as I put out my hand she recoiled with a little cry—without however moving more than a couple of paces.

I could see her now, for my eyes were getting accustomed to the darkness. She was standing hunched forward, with her head down, taking great gulping breaths of air like someone about to faint. I happened to look away for a moment as one does sometimes when trying to think what to do next in some awkward situation. At once she started to shuffle slowly over the carpet in the direction of her room.

If the dead walk, I thought, they must sound like that.

I turned to see whether she needed help and at once the footsteps stopped. I walked closer and she seemed to lean away from me as though unable to take a step in spite of her utmost efforts. Suddenly in a high-pitched voice I should scarcely have recognized as hers had I not seen her standing there she cried, 'Don't touch me; keep away!' and with one hand began to sketch some half familiar gesture on the empty air.

Something seemed momentarily to come between us. When I could see again she was gone. I heard her lock the door of her room and fall on her bed sobbing.

If that had been all I should have left her to sleep off her terrors, for with the best will in the world a man does not relish breaking down his wife's bedroom door in the middle of the night. Besides there was the maid. Marion wouldn't thank me if our night-time adventures were to be plastered across the headlines of the Sunday Press.

Had she done nothing more than cry, I should have gone back to bed; but soon I began to hear a sort of bubbling chuckle break through the sobs at intervals. A sound to freeze the blood, Henry, and only the beginning of it, for very soon it was followed by peal on peal of hysterical laughter.

Earlier I had thought of the effect of our actions on the maid. But now it was too late anyway for secrecy, it seemed to me that the maid might be the answer to the problem. I had to accept the fact, however unwillingly, that for some reason which I could not fathom, Marion believed me to be the cause of her fear. It was obviously better that, until morning brought her less confused thoughts, I should keep as far as possible in the background. Perhaps, I thought, the maid may be able to persuade her to unlock her door, then at least she will have a companion.

The maid's room is in the attic. At one time we had had two maids and a cook living in, but Marion never seemed able to keep servants. Now we had just one middle-aged woman who acted as lady's maid and general help. Other women came by the day: we had our meals brought in from a place down the road.

I blundered around in the attic for several minutes. For some reason it never occurred to me to switch on the lights and I had no idea in which room the woman slept. Finally I found it. She must have shifted in her bed: the springs creaked. I knocked on the door.

At once all sounds ceased from inside and again I was conscious of fear. One's own fears are bad enough, but beyond a certain point they either spur to action—which is a partial relief —or drug one into a state where the finer edges are blunted. But against this fear from *outside* I had no defence.

For a moment I almost turned away and then the absurdity of the thing struck me. Here was a woman I paid to look after my wife and I had come up in a most serious emergency to ask

her to do just that. Why should I, in my own house, steal away
without wakening my own servant simply because she was
afraid of unexpected sounds in the night. The thing to do was,
obviously, to call out and reassure her. Once she heard my voice
the darkness would hold no further terrors for her.

Putting my mouth close to the crack between the door and
the doorpost, I called out gently, 'It's only me, Mr Stephens. I
need your—'

I had not reached the end of the sentence when I was seized
by such a wave of terror that the words were choked in my
throat. It seemed, temporarily, to blot out my capacity to think
—even to perceive what was going on.

Stumbling away from the door as though pursued, it was only
when my distance from it had increased by half the length of
the passage that I became aware of the screaming.

In that echoing attic it seemed to come from all around me.

I needed no one else's fear to urge me now. I leaped down the
stairs crashing against the walls and nearly spraining my ankle
on a loose stair rod. It was only the second flight that pulled me
up, that and the colder air of the hall. We're curiously made,
aren't we? Even in our terrors little bits of civilization cling. By
the time I had reached the hall, I knew I simply couldn't stagger
out into the night in my pyjamas, even if one woman was having
hysterics behind a locked door and another was screaming.

It was in that moment of comparative calm that I realized
there was no longer any sound coming from my wife's room.
That restored my confidence enormously. One of them had
stopped; the most important one, I thought rather brutally.

I tried to get a grip on myself. What ought I to do? Something
should be done to stop the screaming.

The doctor, of course, that was it. I had only to ring and say
there was an emergency, beg him to come at once, murmur
incoherently about fits, and everything would be taken care of.
I didn't mind the idea of going up again with someone else, but
frankly I couldn't face it alone.

The fear, Henry—the maid's, not mine—was what made it
unendurable.

I had reached the light switch and flicked it on. The clock
showed it was just four minutes past twelve. It was not so late
as I had thought, but somehow I couldn't face that bleak

surgical whiteness lights always produce at times when they shouldn't really be lit. I turned them off again and began to work round the hall towards the telephone.

Halfway round I bumped into something that shouldn't have been there. It was tied up in brown paper but there was no mistaking its shape and feel, it was one of those garden trolleys you pull with a walking-stick handle.

I moved on carefully and had almost reached the telephone when, suddenly, it rang.

What happened then, happened so quickly that it only remains in my mind like a ghastly hallucination. That bell ringing must have been the last straw for the maid. She went mad. I felt her go mad, Henry. Can you imagine the horror of such a thing happening inside your head? No, you can't; no one could. Every hold I had on reality broke loose.

This time the image of fear was so potent that words came with it. I heard them repeated again and again in my mind as if they were being shouted aloud—'They know; they've found out!' They were words of mortal terror, and yet I had no knowledge then—as I have none now—of what they meant.

All this appeared to take place in a time both instantaneously short and infinitely long, a time that had no reality in human terms.

I don't know what happened then. I remember running, falling, a softness, nothing more.

When I came to, it was light. I was in my bed. That must have been the softness. I got up. Surprisingly there were no bruises on me; I felt no strains, no stiffness. Walking very quietly over to Marion's door I gently tried the handle. I dared not knock.

The door was unlocked. I heard Marion's voice say sleepily, 'Who's that?' There was no hint of fear in it. Perhaps the morning light had shown her the foolishness of her behaviour.

I walked in, looking for some reaction that would tell me where to go from there. She just lay looking at me as though it were any other morning.

She knew *nothing*, Henry, *absolutely nothing* of what had happened.

It was the same with the maid. I didn't need to ask either of them: I could see it. Whatever had happened, it had not happened for them and therefore, logically, it *had not happened for me*.

Is sanity just agreeing with enough people about enough things? Over a good breakfast I was honestly beginning to wonder whether it hadn't all been a dream, vivid though the memories were, and then I saw what Marion was holding.

It was a catalogue of garden equipment.

I was determined not to cheat by asking a leading question. Quite casually I leaned across the table. 'Are you thinking of buying anything from those people?' I asked. 'I believe they're quite good,' I added so that she would not have to waste time being defensive.

'Yes,' she said, 'I've decided to get one of these; just the thing for dead-heading and weeding,' and she showed me a picture of the trolley I had fallen over the night before.

You know me, Henry, I don't believe in guesswork. I checked with Marion. I checked with the maid and the gardener and all the casuals. There had never been a trolley just like that anywhere in the place—even on loan. The railway van had never delivered such a thing. The makers had never had such an order from our address and they only sold directly to the public—it had never happened.

Well, there it is. You've a logical mind; I don't have to tell you the answer.

Marion has put her order in the post today. I've checked in another name how long the firm will take to effect delivery.

Ten days, they say. In ten days I shan't be alive. That's the maximum time I've got to live.

Last night—I have to call it that—last night when I woke up it was ten days on from now, the package had arrived and I was *dead*. It's the only answer, Henry. It fits all the facts, the panic, my knowing what they felt, the odd sensation when I got up, even the dislike of the light. You see now why you must come at once. It may happen any time before that.

Marion took it so well. I hadn't thought she cared so much. I only told her a little, just about seeing her and the trolley. My noticing the time helped to convince her it wasn't just nonsense. She's been extraordinarily brave. Now it's up to us. I've simply got to draw up that new will in time and you've got to help me. We must see that justice is done.

> Yours as ever,
> Bob.

That was Bob Stephens's letter; a strange document. But justice it seems was done by it. This morning, early, I had a telephone call from the Stephens's maid to say that her mistress had had to be removed some hours previously to an asylum. The girl sounded extremely upset. Apparently both of them received some great shock in the night and it must have proved too much for Mrs Stephens's imagination. The last words the girl had heard from her before she became incoherent had been shouted in the night. 'They know,' she had screamed, 'they've found out!'

I was glad then that I had guessed correctly, for in reading Bob's letter certain things had struck me as odd and it was because of them that I had made my seemingly unnecessary telephone call in reply to the request of a dead man. Granted, as his letter seemed to prove, that he had genuinely experienced while living the appearance he was to make in the house ten days later—after his death—and several questions at once arose demanding answer. Why had his wife been out on the landing at all at that hour? And if the meeting were fortuitous, why had she deliberately chosen to confront his 'ghost'? Not for love, it seemed by her questions, but to get confirmation as to whether he remembered something. 'Do you know what has happened?' had been her question. But what was there that he could have known before his death that she would not also have known? He mentioned nothing of this importance in his letter—and it was the final letter of a man putting his affairs in order before certain death.

There could have been only one reason for her asking such a question in spite of her manifest terror—the need to be sure that he did *not* remember something she had done, something whose enormity caused her to fear that he might trouble her even from beyond the grave itself.

It was obvious to me that she had killed him.

The cry 'They know; they've found out!' had been *hers* not the maid's. She, after all, was much the nearer of the two to the ringing telephone. Bob had noted that the emanations of terror he received from the maid rapidly decreased in strength as he moved away from her though, fatally for himself, he had failed to draw the obvious deduction from his observation.

My telephone call must have seemed to his wife's taut nerves the first sign that justice was catching up with her. Bob had not mentioned that part of the dream to her and who but the police would ring at such an hour?

I doubt whether we shall ever find out how she killed her husband. That she did I am absolutely certain, but what would I produce as evidence? And what need of evidence is there when justice has, so manifestly, been done? Guilt is a terrible thing.

Nightmare

BERLIE DOHERTY

Rab lives over the railway lines, near the allotments. He doesn't always live there; sometimes I don't see him for weeks or even months, and then he just turns up again as if he's never been away. He lives in an old shed that needs pulling down—it's more of a barn, really with high heavy doors. He says it's all that's left of his estate, that long ago his family lived in a big house that was bombed in the war, and that all the allotments are really on his land. His grandad's a horse-dealer; they go round the country together to horse fairs and markets. I don't think Rab gets to school much; he's supposed to go to the one by the allotments when they're here, but I don't think he's got a lot of time for that sort of learning. They're a bit like gypsies, really. I'm not supposed to have anything to do with him, but I do. I can't help it. If you knew Rab you'd understand.

He hangs round and waits for me to come over the hill from

school, and I see him leaning against the big chestnut tree or sitting astride the wall near our house and I think, Great! Rab's back!

I wish he hadn't come this winter though.

'Coming on moors?' he asks me, as if I only saw him yesterday. 'Coming up to Downpour?' And before I know it I've run in to change into old clothes that I'm allowed to get mucky, and I'm racing over the moors with him, scrambling over those massive boulders that he says are fossilized dinosaur droppings, and slithering behind the waterfall to the dark cave behind it that we call the Downpour Den. 'Cavemen lived here,' he tells me, and his voice bounces round the dripping hollows. 'You're standing on the dust of their bones.' I know it's true. 'We'd be all right here, if there was a Big Bang. We could come here and live.'

Rab isn't a house person. He isn't much older than me, but he knows everything. I'm sure that's because he isn't a house person. He lives in the hut with his grandad, Ged, who's a grimy-looking cold and sour fellow; he never speaks to me; I'm not sure I like him at all. And when they feel like going they just go. I hate it. I never know they've gone. I go down to their hut and try to peer in through the one high window, but they have stringy curtains draped across and there's nothing to see in there. There's a smell of Rab and Ged though, whether they're there or not. People have tried to get that hut knocked down while they're away, but they can't. It belongs to Rab and his grandad. It's their home.

'I wish you wouldn't go without telling me,' I say to him. 'I hate that, not saying goodbye and that.'

That always makes him laugh. 'What's the point of saying goodbye?' he says. 'I know I'll be coming back.'

Last time Rab turned up was in the dead of last winter. I wish I hadn't seen him. It was after Christmas, and I was just going up our road to the post and there he was, hunched up in the cold by the chestnut tree. The snow had come a few days before and now it was packed ice.

It was an effort to walk upright.

'All right, Rab?' I shouted, pleased to see him, but not showing it.

'Coming up to Downpour?' he asked me.

'Eh, it's freezing!' I said. 'We'll never get over moors in this lot.'

'Get your boots on,' he told me, not even looking at me, holding his white hands up to his mouth as though he was trying to melt his fingers with his breath. 'See you at moorgates. There's something I want to tell you.'

I always do what Rab says. I can't help it. Half an hour later I'd got my thickest clothes on and my boots and I was standing by the white stile that leads off up to the open moorland, stamping on a patch of ice that was iron-hard. Nothing moved. The sun was lemon-yellow but there was no heat from it at all, and all the blades of grass and bells of dead heather were clamped in their own ice-shells.

I heard Rab whistle, and I saw him come out onto the footpath about a quarter of a mile on from where I was standing. I waved and swung myself over the stile, lost my footing on the last slippery step and sprawled head first into the ice-blades. By the time I'd picked myself up Rab was out of sight, but I knew the way off by heart and slithered after him, my heart jerking into my throat every time I lost my footing.

I caught up with him at the Edge. He was sitting with his legs dangling over a drop of nearly a hundred foot, looking out across the deep white floor of the valley. I eased myself onto the slab next to him. In summer you can hear the curlews up here, and the cackling of the grouse on the moors, and the sheep yelling to each other across the slopes, but today, when my panting had died down, there was nothing. Not a sound.

'Everything's died,' I said.

'The winter solstice,' Rab said. 'Everything's standing still. The sun, and the grass, and the streams, and the birds. Nothing moving.'

'You'd think it was waiting for something.'

'There's nothing to wait for now. It's too late.'

You don't expect Rab to sound like that, with that kind of sadness in his voice. He pulled himself up and spat over the Edge. We listened out for the tiny splat as it struck rock, and laughed. That was more like it.

'Gozzing's good for you,' he told me. 'Clears your passages. If you swallow your gozz it clogs up all your works.'

He set off carefully over a boulder that was completely cased in ice, and then started running, his boots striking the iron of the ground like flints, a kind of urgency; I lost sight of him as he ran and could only hear the chime of his stride, and then I heard nothing but my own steps as I stumbled and slid, and the rapid rasp of my breath.

I skidded at last down the slope to the Downpour, and brought myself to a halt against the squat stone we called toad-rock. From here the narrow track twists round and comes below the cascading force of the waterfall. Because of the twist of the valley you don't hear anything from this side of toad-rock. As soon as you scramble round it to the jut of the path you're deafened by its clamour; it drowns out everything, and the spray from it showers over you—no escaping till you ease yourself behind it into the den.

I edged myself round the glassy rock-foot, and then I was struck by the weight of silence. The whole waterfall was frozen—I could see great limbs of icicles sprouting from the overhang, and the green-white sheen of a huge slab of ice draped across the mouth of Downpour Den, like a curtain. The silence was heavier than the noise I'd expected—it was like a pressure waiting to burst, waiting to explode into splinters and tumble down the boulder scree to the valley.

Rab was clinging onto a rock near the overhang, and I made my way over to him, hugging the slippery skin of the stones with both hands as I went; but when I reached him and looked up at last into the frozen curtain that hung over the Downpour I saw something that was so terrifying that I'll never get it out of my mind, that I think of every day, as if it's part of me now. It was this: a horse, trapped in the ice; a great black horse, its legs straddled so its hooves were planted firmly in bed-rock, its head lifted, teeth bared in fright, its eyes staring; locked in death.

I think I crawled back up on my hands and knees till I was on ground where I felt safe enough to stand, and then I started running, feet splaying out each side of me, my head pounding and dizzy; when I couldn't breathe any more I turned round to wait for Rab, but he was nowhere in sight. I could have sworn I'd heard him scrabbling back up the slope after me, and the thud of his boots on the hard rocks. I waited a bit but the cold began to seep into me; I couldn't stop myself from shaking, still in shock from the sight of the horse frozen into its glassy tomb.

Besides, Rab knew many routes over the moors—he could be anywhere. I jogged back home, glad of the comforting warmth of our house, and the quiet normal talking of my mum and dad in the kitchen.

I couldn't sleep that night. Mum had gone to bed early and Dad was playing his jazz in the front room. Usually I love to listen to music when I'm in bed; in the end it always drowses me off to sleep. I went downstairs and got myself a drink, then wandered into the back room. We don't use that room much in winter; it's a cold room, because we're on the edge of town and the wind comes off the moors onto the back of the house, and we made the mistake of putting big sliding door-windows in to give us a better view.

I went over to the window now. The curtain had been pulled across to keep out the draught, but I thought I'd like to look at the moors in the moonlight, the blue-white gleam of the snow. Just before I reached the window I heard Rab's voice, calling my name very softly from outside. It was almost as if I'd known he'd be there.

I tugged at the curtain with one hand, sipping at my hot chocolate, and there instead of the sliding window was a huge slab of ice, and frozen into it, the black horse.

Its eyes were wide open and its ears pressed back, and its yellow teeth were bared in fright. As I watched in the same lock of fear it reared back its head. In slow motion its front legs carved an upwards arc and flung black hooves to pound against the ice; I could hear the sweet breathy sound of the saxophone in the other room, and I could hear the pounding of the hooves, and the ice tearing in front of me, above and around me, the splintering and crinkling as a thousand tiny bright shards showered over me, sharp as glass, bright as water. Hooves flailed as the black horse reared again, with hot life snorting from his nostrils. And clinging on to his back, laughing down at me, was Rab.

'Come on!' he shouted. 'Up on moors.' He leaned down, one arm tucked into the horse's mane, and heaved me up in front of him.

I can feel the way my legs ached as they stretched across the black sinewy back, and the lurching sensation beneath me as we galloped over the moors. I'd never ridden a horse in my life,

and I was jolted from side to side and up and down with the unfamiliar movement. Rab had his arm round my waist to stop me from slipping off, and I remember the ice-cold pressure of his fingers.

I dug my fingers into the mane and clung onto it; it felt like thick, silky hair. The air on my cheeks was raw, and as we plunged into the black bitter night, away from the houses, away from the lights, I felt as if all my known world was slipping away from me; and that this was where I'd rather be, riding forever in cold air. We soared over the white stile of moorgates and thundered up the familiar whitened tracks, with the stars hanging and turning like icicles. Gleaming boulders loomed up and away from us. We were streaming fast, floating; we were in a different element, like water.

I recognized the squat bulk of the toad-stone, where the scree slope fell away from us; I recognized the splintered ice-curtain of the Downpour, and as the horse leapt across the mouth of it into the black cavern behind I tried to slide off his back . . .

'No!' I screamed. 'Not there!'

Rab laughed, his ice-cold hands pressing into my ribs, and his laugh echoed and bounced in the hollows of the caves. 'Stay with me,' he urged. 'Don't leave me.'

I heard a creaking above my head, and watched the slow languorous curtain of ice slide down to envelop the cave, felt the intense chill of it as it scraped across my skin, trapping me . . .

My dad found me standing in the dark in the back room. He took the cup of cold chocolate out of my hand.

'You've had a nightmare,' he said. 'You're all right.'

I jerked back the curtain, expecting to find the window shattered, and the snow on the lawn outside swirled round with the kicking of hooves, but there was nothing to see, only the moors cold and quiet in the moonlight, and the stars, like twisting icicles.

'There was a horse,' I told Dad. 'It carried me off to the Downpour . . .'

He led me back upstairs to my room. 'People used to think,' he told me, 'that wild horses came in the night and carried them off to terrible places. That's why it's called a nightmare. Go to sleep now. You'll be all right.'

But I had no intentions of sleeping ever again. I sat bolt upright in my bed with the light on, listening out for the stamp of hooves on the iron earth, and for Rab. Laughing.

The next day was the beginning of the new term. It stayed just below freezing all day, but the sun was bright and the sky was a kind of fierce blue. It was the sort of day that Rab and I liked to go up on the moors, when you could see for miles from the Edge, all the little villages and roads in the valley, and the river winding slowly through.

I couldn't get Rab off my mind that day. I wanted to tell him about my dream. I wondered if he'd had the same one. We'd tried to do that many times—we'd told each other that we would try to dream the same thing, and meet up in our dreams. We'd nearly done it once—we'd both dreamt of the Downpour Den one night, but there'd been no people in either of our dreams. Why had he laughed, in my dream? Why had he wanted to be trapped in the ice-cave, when I'd been so frightened? And even as I thought of all these things that I wanted to ask him about, the idea came to me just as powerfully as it had done last night, that it hadn't been a dream at all, but that it had really happened.

And there was another thing that bothered me. When we'd gone up to the Downpour yesterday he'd said there was something he wanted to tell me. He'd taken me to see the horse, but he hadn't told me anything, except that it was the winter solstice. I knew that. I knew that we'd had midwinter's night before Christmas, and that it was as if nothing grew around that time, waiting for the sun to move nearer our part of the earth again. '*It's too late.*' That was what he'd said.

I had to stay behind after school to help get all last term's art work down from the walls, and by the time I left it was nearly dark. I hurried down to the allotments. It was bitterly cold down there, directly exposed to the moors, and there was very little light left. The town lights were behind me. I picked my way along the path. A stray cat yowled at me from its ratting place near the whitened mound of the compost heap. I found my way by memory to the high bulk of Rab's shed, and I could tell that it was in darkness.

I went up to it all the same, and tried to peer in through the high curtained window. Surely they hadn't gone again so soon? I was just about to move away when I heard a movement inside; a kind of hollow knocking. 'Rab?' I shouted. 'You in there?' There was silence, but then the knocking came again; but it wasn't knocking at all, it was stamping, and I knew the sound from the farmers' yards down in the valley. It was the impatient clopping sound of a horse's hooves. I backed away, and the stamping began again, more urgent this time. The high wooden door of the hut shook, and I knew that the horse inside was rearing up against it, beating its hooves, trying to tear it down.

'Stop it!' I shouted, hardly realizing what I was doing. 'I know what you are. You're not a horse at all. You're only a nightmare.'

I started to run, skidding on the slippery path as I went. But how could it be a nightmare, when the lights of my town were blinking like low yellow stars in front of me, and I could hear the drone of cars making for the motorway? Behind me was the thundering of hooves pounding on wood, and the terrible splintering as the door began to give way.

I ran wildly towards the warm familiar town lights, and as the path turned to stubbed grass and then met the pavement I skidded on the ice, fell headlong and closed my eyes, wanting to sleep . . .

'All right, love? Come on. Up you get. No bones broken.'

Davey Brown, an old friend of my dad's, hauled me up and brushed me down.

'You're shaking like a plate of jelly. Come on, get in my car, and I'll run you home. I want a word with your dad anyway, about the new allotment hut . . . In you get.'

I was glad of his offer. Davey had left the engine running when he stopped to help me up, and the car was still warm.

'Good job I saw you fall,' he said, as we pulled away into the traffic. 'You must have been going at quite a pace to come down like that. Shouldn't run on ice, you know.'

'I saw a horse,' I said. 'It scared me.'

'A horse?'

'I didn't exactly see it,' I added. 'I heard it. On the allotments.'

He shook his head. 'I doubt it. How would a horse get there? Whereabouts on the allotments?'

It felt safer now, in the warmth of the car. It was comforting to be told that I must have imagined it. I didn't mind if he laughed at me. I wanted to be brought away from the nightmare.

'I thought I heard it,' I said, 'in the hut.'

'But there isn't a hut,' Davey said. 'Not any more.'

Not any more. I began to shiver violently again now. Nightmare and reality became one thing, as I walked again in my memory down the dark track, past the cat crouching in the hedge, saw the looming shape of the hut, peered through the window, touched the wood of the door . . .

'We pulled it down over the weekend,' Davey went on. 'Real eyesore, that thing. That's why I'm wanting a word with your dad about building us a dry, secure little hut for the allotment users to keep their tools and seeds and things in. We've been wanting one on that site for years . . .'

We waited for the traffic lights to change. Was I really in Davey's car, I wondered, or was I still lying on the ice, or peering through the hut window, or chasing Rab over the moors, or looking at the frozen slab of the Downpour . . .

'But it's their home,' I managed to say, trying to get him to talk again. As long as Davey talked, surely I was in the car next to him, safe and warm, and on my way home. 'They live there.'

'Old Ged? He came up a few days ago. He wanted to collect a few bits and pieces that he'd left behind. But he'll not be coming back, he said. Not without the lad. I expect your mum and dad told you, didn't they? Terrible business, that.'

We had arrived at our house. I followed him down the jennel and into the kitchen. Mum sat me down by the radiator and gave me a hot drink and got on with preparing the meal while my dad and Davey worked out a price agreement for the hut they were wanting on the allotments. I went out into the back room while they were talking, and I drew back the heavy curtains and looked out across the dark plain of the moors. Something outside was dripping, very slowly, very softly.

My mother came in and stood beside me.

'Shall I tell you about Rab?' she said.

Dread slowed the pumping of my blood.

'Listen,' I said. 'It's thawing.'

'Yes. The forecast said temperatures would go up tonight.' She touched my arm. 'I thought you and Rab had stopped seeing each other years ago. That's why I didn't tell you.'

'Rab was my best friend,' I said.

I didn't look at her while she was telling me. I didn't listen to her. I knew already what had happened to him. I listened instead to Rab and myself talking quietly together, sitting next to each other on the Edge, the day he showed me the frozen horse.

'Everything's died.'

'The winter solstice. Everything's standing still. The sun, and the grass, and the streams, and the birds. Nothing moving.'

'You'd think it was waiting for something.'

'There's nothing to wait for now. It's too late.'

'Rab was killed about three weeks ago,' my mother was saying. 'He stole a ride on somebody's horse, and it took fright and threw him. He died on midwinter's day. The longest night of the year.'

The dripping from the roof had turned into a trickle. I could see it coursing down the outside of the window; ice running free again. Tomorrow the Downpour would crack and burst and gush back to life. But I would never see Rab again. I thought of him, a free spirit, urging the black horse on over the moors, riding free, laughing.

'I already knew that,' I said to her. 'Rab came back to tell me.'

The Big Wind

MARIEN DREYER

Mallory felt, rather than heard, the explosion. It was a far-off sensation of great movement and, when he opened his eyes, he went out on to the balcony of his mountain shack and looked around to see if there was any indication of what had happened.

It was almost sunrise. The sky was pink under the clouds, like a galah's breast. He looked at the sky for a moment or two before realization came that he was facing west and that it was 5 a.m. by his watch.

Mallory fled through the house to the kitchen, which faced east, and saw the sun rising there. Back he went to the other side of the house to see a second sun hanging in the sky.

There was no doubt about it. Two suns were rising in the sky, now streaked with sullen cloud, fiery cloud that should have been a steel wool grey, but was bloodshot with scarlet, like clouds over a bushfire.

To make quite sure, Mallory climbed up on to the roof and so removed any possible doubt. He saw two suns rising, one east, one west. And fear took him in its grip. He slid down the roof and went into the kitchen to make himself a pot of coffee.

There had been little rain for some months, so he had not the water to spare for a shower, only for a quick splash and shave.

When he went back to the balcony, the curious sight had gone. The clouds made it impossible to see the sun or suns; but they were still redly angry.

Mallory drank his coffee and considered the phenomenon. Undoubtedly there had been another atomic device detonated, and that had probably caused a refraction of the sun on the clouds as it rose. At all events, the sky seemed normal enough again.

Mallory's cabin sat on the top of a mountain. In winter it was snow-bound and he could not get near it, but in late spring, all summer, and early autumn he went up there most weekends, leaving his car at the township down the mountain and climbing the rest of the way on foot.

He had carried everything he needed to build the shack up the mountain, using a pack-horse for the heavier components of the hut, and it had taken him several years to build it.

There, he could be alone and relax in the silence. Dixie, his wife, came up once but decided it was too remote and too hard to get there, so she did not come again.

The hut was small, but soundly built and comfortable. The only life he saw there was an occasional eagle hovering high up. At night, the stars were low and brilliant, and Mallory looked forward to going up to his retreat. Working as he did in advertising all the week, he needed the solitude and peace and high places near the sky to let his mind become restored to sanity. In the hut, he drew and painted the things he wanted to do without regard for advertisers.

After he had his coffee, he sat out on the balcony and worked on a drawing, wondering with part of his mind why there should have been two suns. He had almost expected to hear the Last Trumpet sound—he imagined that this would be a sweet, clear, unearthly note, but on reflection decided that Gabriel would be au fait with the modern idiom and would swing it.

When he first heard the noise there was nothing sweet and

clear about it. It was a screaming, rushing howl, and before he had had a chance to move the wind hit. It came from nowhere and in a blast that made the cottage shudder. Mallory's drawings went—he never saw them again.

Mallory had to crawl around the balcony to the back door, go in and use all his strength to close the western door and bar it. He had to bar the shutters on his crawl around, and the wind flattened him against the walls. It was like being hit by a pile driver, blow after blow, the impact was so strong.

Eventually, when he did bar the shutters, the only way to get back was to drop on all fours, and flatten out like an insect, worming his way back into shelter. There was not a wind gauge at the shack, but Mallory thought it must have been a squall in excess of one hundred miles per hour. He began to feel afraid—an unreasoning, irrational fear.

That was the Saturday morning, and the wind screamed and tore at the cottage all that day and all that night. Mid-morning on Sunday it stopped as suddenly as it had come. Mallory left the shutters barred, locked the hut door, and set off down to the township. The silence was painful after the roar of the wind and its pressure on his eardrums.

There was evidence of the wind all the way down the side of the mountain. Huge trees, centuries old, had been uprooted and sprawled across the rough track, roots bare of soil, naked and hideous like a newly extracted tooth. He did not see any small trees—they had ceased to be, and he could only think that they had been blown away completely. The earth was pock-marked as if it had been under concentrated shellfire.

When Mallory reached the service station he was sweating, and not from heat. It was a relief to find the place was safe, but it was on the eastern side of the little mountain, and old Steve, who ran the service station, said: 'Bad bit of wind, Dick.'

'Pretty fierce,' allowed Mallory carefully. 'Did you see the sky yesterday morning?'

'Yair—looked as if a storm was coming up.' Steve said nothing about the two suns, and Mallory did not mention it nor press for any information. He wanted to get back to his family.

'That's what I thought,' he said. 'I think I'll head for home while it's clear.'

'Ah, well,' philosophized Steve, 'messing around with those bombs. Mucking all the weather up. They let one off late on Friday, it said on the radio yesterday morning.'

'Yes,' said Mallory. 'Well, I better get moving.'

He drove much faster than was his custom, and as he reached level country, he saw the wind had left its mark.

Fences were down and trees were flattened, power lines were snarled in a tangle, and as he went on through the semi-rural areas, there were houses which had been unroofed and in some cases quite demolished. Gangs of men were working on power lines, and emergency helpers were trying to straighten out the wreckage of homes. He had to detour more than once to let heavy machinery through, and thought of stopping to help but the driving urgency to get home made him go faster.

Unreasoning panic gripped him again and when he had to detour off the main highway to let through maintenance trucks and equipment, and trucks bearing emergency food and clothing, he fumed with rage.

His own home, facing a beach, had been protected by a hilly crest behind it. When he garaged the car and went inside, Dixie looked at him anxiously. 'You're back early,' she said. 'What brought that on?' but relief belied the lightness of her words and voice.

'The wind,' he said softly, an irrational fear in his mind that the wind might come back if he spoke loudly. 'It was pretty fierce up at the shack. I wanted to be sure everything was all right here.'

Dixie shuddered. 'It was awful here,' she said, speaking softly too. 'We haven't any lights yet, and the phone went.'

As she spoke, the phone hiccuped, and Mallory picked it up. It was his partner, Arthur Vickers, calling. 'Just ringing to see if Dixie and the kids are all right,' he said. 'Didn't expect to get you.'

'I came back to see if everything was safe,' said Mallory. 'Are you all right?'

'Fairly so,' said Vickers. 'We're halfway down a gully, you know, and on the western side. People on top and on the side opposite copped the lot.'

Mallory noted with a corner of his mind that Vickers was speaking barely above a whisper too. 'We're taking in about half a dozen kids,' said Vickers. 'Their houses were wrecked, so until their families get things straight, we'll take the kids. It was a corker while it lasted. I never knew anything like it before.'

'Nor I,' whispered Mallory. 'See you in the morning.'

When he hung up, Dixie looked at him steadily. 'What's on your mind?'

He told her about the two suns rising in the sky and wished he hadn't. She shivered. 'Dick—I'm scared . . .' she whispered, her face creasing like a child's with terror.

'So am I,' he said in that soft, odd half whisper. 'But let's not panic. Where are the kids?'

'Out helping to fix up the wrecked houses,' said Dixie. The boys came in about an hour later, bubbling over with stories of the hurricane, and with two fourteen year olds—Don and Desmond were twins—tumbling around the house, the Fear retreated a little.

Until the 7 p.m. news. The calm and unemotional voice of the announcer told of tremendous seas in the Tasman and hurricanes in New Zealand. Mallory felt the blood draining from his face. He picked up the terrestrial globe and traced his finger around the line of latitude to see where it passed.

'In twenty-four hours it'll hit South America,' he said. 'They'll cop it in Chile, the Argentine, and Uruguay. About Thursday, there'll be records of hurricanes in South Africa. It's due in Western Australia on Saturday . . .'

'And back for Sunday dinner with us,' said Desmond, the junior twin. Don pooh-poohed the idea as unscientific and impossible.

'You might be right,' said Mallory, not specifying which twin he answered.

In the first news broadcast for Tuesday there was word of a disastrous hurricane devastating South America. The kids stared at their father. He said nothing but came home at midday, not in his car, but in a utility truck. He had loaded up the truck with tinned foods of every kind and had several drums of kerosene and a first aid chest. In the bottom of the tray, he had four heavy steel cables, and eight thick dog spikes.

The boys came home from school for lunch and he set them digging pits six feet deep, two on each side of the house.

'But why?' asked Don.

'Because we're going to anchor the house,' said Mallory. 'I'm going to put the dog spikes on to the end of the cables, bury the spikes in the ground, and there'll be a concrete truck along presently to fill them up with concrete. The cables are going over the roof—get digging.'

They got digging. Dixie lent a hand, and by the time the truck came, they were ready. The driver and his offsider grinned, but the Mallorys took no notice.

'Hope it holds,' said Mallory, looking at a limpid evening sky.

Midday on Thursday, there was a broadcast of a catastrophic hurricane sweeping across South Africa. The kids no longer looked rather pityingly at their parent—they just stared at him thoughtfully, wondering . . .

He came home on Friday morning with steel sheeting, drilled holes in it and nailed it to the windows facing west. The boys helped, not asking why or what, just helping without any argument or comment.

On Saturday morning the sky was lucent blue and clear, as it should be in early autumn, the wind light and nor'-west. People who passed the fortified house stopped to stare, even to smile tolerantly, and when noon came and the sky was still clear, Mallory felt a little abashed at his own hasty panic.

However, he went ahead with his preparations, filling the bath with water, making the boys fill sandbags which he put around the western wall, and ignoring the comments of neighbours. The first race description on the radio was just beginning when the interruption came. A news flash. 'Catastrophic hurricane hits Western Australia . . .'

That calm, professionally unemotional voice had a tinge of shocked terror to it. They had little information because all communications had been broken. All that was known was that a terrific wind had hit the western coast, along with a tidal wave, and after that, there had been no further news from the western coast.

It was expected, the announcer said in an edged voice, that the storm would reach the eastern States within twenty-four hours. Listeners would be kept informed. It was then just after noon.

Mallory heard the wind coming just before six. One moment the seaside suburb was as quiet as could be expected on a

Saturday night when the youngsters were going home from the beach. He heard the high, terrifying noise coming, and he raced into the the street to get as many children as he could to safety. He had planned with Don and Des to play a crazy game of follow my leader, and to bring them in to the protected house as soon as he gave the signal.

In doing that, he got almost forty children inside. They were crowded, but safe, and for the next ten hours it was just noise. Ear splitting, incredible noise. A scream that never ceased. The children were afraid initially, but accepted things placidly, as children do. They were under cover and had plenty of food, the two adults caring for them were familiar figures—it was logical to stay in a safe place until the storm spent itself. Mallory and his wife fed them, organized games, and community singing, and kept them as busy as possible. When it grew late, the kids placidly accepted the fact that they would sleep with the Mallorys and go home later. There was no panic.

Early next morning, just after dawn, Mallory went to the far side of the house facing the eastern sky, and in that first light rubbed his eyes and stared again. Most of the children still slept. Some of the older boys and girls were awake, talking quietly to Dixie and the twins. Mallory looked over as Dixie, sensing his shock, looked in his direction and she obeyed the slight movement of his head to come. She joined him at the windows, staring, her face wiped of any feeling.

Ordinarily the view was of tossing water, lapis lazuli waves curling over into white frills on yellow sand, but there was no sea any more—only sand for as far as they could see as if the sea had been pushed back by a colossal squeegee. No sea, only sand blowing in clouds.

At six, the wind had gone and it was quiet again, very still and quiet. More frightening, this stillness after the scream of the big wind. Terrifying to ears now attuned to noise. The sea crept back timidly, finding its way through new hillocks of sand, lapping apologetically along the beach.

Mallory went out through the kitchen door and round to what had been the street. There wasn't anything left except his own house, anchored with the cables and spikes into the concrete. Bits of debris were banked up against the sandbagged wall of the Mallory house. There was nothing else. The children came out slowly and quietly, not talking or saying anything, just looking numbly. Mallory found things banked up against the wall of his house—things that had once been human and were now only shards of flesh and shreds of bone. They were unidentifiable scraps of people.

Mallory looked at it all, and pointed back to the house. The children went in without argument. 'No use rebuilding or trying to find anything,' he said to Dixie. 'It will come back again—earlier this time. Probably about Thursday.'

They went back to the children who sat, waiting. Mallory told them what had happened without trying to gloss it over. The older ones were sober and conscious of the tragedy, the younger ones could not comprehend fully what had happened, but he told them simply what he thought.

'You can stay here,' he said. 'If there are any survivors, we'll find them.'

There was not any radio any more. There were special emergency editions of newspapers, but they had little because there were no longer any communication facilities. The cables across the sea beds had gone, radio towers no longer existed. There was nothing left.

Mallory drove through the wreckage to the northern suburb in which Vickers lived. Vickers and his family were safe—they had survived the big wind, and were sheltering children whom they had found. Some of his neighbours had survived, and they came together as a group to work out what to do.

Only then did Mallory tell of the two suns he had seen rising.

'I feel,' he said in the low voice they all used now, 'that we ought to find enough people to come with us. I know there are caves at the foot of the mountain where I have my weekend shack. If we can get up to the caves—take as many people as we can get, as much equipment and supplies as we can get—we'll be safe there until we can work out what to do.'

'Go underground until it stops?' said Vickers. 'Dick—what if it doesn't stop?'

'Have to face that,' said Mallory dourly. 'We don't know what will happen, but I estimate it will be back on Thursday. You organize things on this side—I'll do my part on my side. I'll get in touch with you on Friday.'

Mallory went home, collecting people on the way. They were

dazed, but willing to help in spite of the stupor. He set them to searching the wreckage for tinned food, and crammed as many people as he could into his house.

The big wind came back late on Wednesday night and blew for sixteen hours. Mallory calculated that the next time it would be on the Monday—it was about thirty-six hours earlier each time, and he did not dwell on what would happen when the thirty-six hour time lag caught up with the wind.

They worked without stopping, Vickers and Mallory and all the people they had found, the children—everybody. Mallory had found doctors and dentists, engineers, teachers, men who had always been in labouring jobs and men who could handle cars. There were others, men and women they had found looting the stores and who were unprepared to come and unwanted by the others.

They were ready early on the Sunday, and Mallory thought— when he had time to think—that they were akin to Noah, only they were on wheels. They had found trucks in underground garages, and they had found cattle and horses, and poultry which had survived. They took only those things which helped them to build and make other things, disregarding all the unessentials.

Dixie led the way in the utility with Don and Des. Armed. Each passenger beside the driver of each truck was armed, and there was not a car in the motorcade. Only trucks. Mallory prized one item on a heavy low loader—the bank buildings, the solid granite bank buildings had gone, but he had found the door to the safe deposit. Vickers had found the low loader and a heavy duty crane. This was in the centre of the motorcade. The heavy metal door would seal off the caves against the wind, so long as it kept on coming from the west.

Bumper to bumper, the odd procession made all speed after Dixie, over what had once been homes and factories and parks and gardens, now all flattened and rubble. They had food for six months, Mallory calculated. They had people to help them survive. After that, he did not know.

There were some who had escaped but were too shocked and numb to care, who sat in tears waiting for somebody to come and do all the work of rebuilding, but unwilling to do it themselves. Mallory left them behind.

Exactly what they would do in the caves, he did not know. All he knew was that he had to hurry, and he had given orders that if one truck broke down, the ones behind were to push. They had perhaps thirty-six hours in which to get into the caves and established before the big wind came back.

The state of the roads and the varied types of trucks in the convoy slowed their speed, so the journey took six hours. Mallory could do it as a rule in two hours. Amongst their essentials was a portable lighting plant, and though they were all weary to death, Mallory and Vickers kept everybody working at top speed, unloading and storing their supplies, and the tougher members of the party used the steel supports Mallory had remembered to bring to shore up the mouth of the cave, and then—last thing they did—they offloaded the solid steel door and set it into place.

As they closed it, Mallory heard the familiar, terrifying howl as the wind swept down the mountain, and he welcomed the smooth workmanship of the door as it slid fast. The concussion of its closure was as if some high explosive had shut off the world . . .

Mallory could feel the concussion. It sounded far off, but distinct, except that it was not so much sound as a feeling of being hit by something, and the silence was deafening in his ears. He had the feeling of great and unearthly power unleashed . . .

He had closed his eyes as the big wind came. He could feel the silent shock waves, and he opened his eyes to see how the others were taking it—and saw the familiar print on the wall at the end of his bed in his shack.

For a few moments, he was dazed and shaking, panting like a man who has been running hard and fast and had come to his last gasp. He closed his eyes and opened them again for the sheer pleasure of seeing the quiet familiarity of his shack, as reassuring as his mother's voice and arms when he had suffered from childhood nightmares. It was all perfectly normal, and he shuddered, rubbing his eyes to push away the terrible horror he had endured in his mind.

He went into the kitchen to get the brandy he kept there for emergencies and poured himself a stiff drink—almost a tumbler full. He was facing the window, which faced east. The sun was just rising, the clouds sullen and grey bloodshot with red, like bushfire smoke at dusk.

He took the brandy in his hand and walked hesitatingly through to the balcony to prove that the whole thing had been a horrendous nightmare, and to reassure himself that he was at last awake. He looked out across the heavily timbered gully over the top of the next mountain, and there, as he had seen it happen, the sun also rose. Rose in the west, with clouds sullen grey streaked with blood red as he had seen them.

He stood there, shuddering, staring and wondering. Terribly afraid. Hopelessly, irrationally afraid . . .

Four Twenty-four Precisely

JOHN EDGELL

Young Alan Clark was travelling by train between Paddington Station and Cardiff one wintry afternoon, when an odd thing happened.

About one hour out of Paddington an elderly man entered the compartment in which Alan was seated alone. He carried a black bag and had the pale skin of a clerk who sat in badly ventilated offices away from the sunlight and fresh air. He sat down opposite Alan and took a newspaper from his bag which he opened and read.

Alan, who noticed nothing strange about the man, looked out of the window. The countryside, rather bleak and pitted with the effects of industry, slipped quickly past. The afternoon sky was darkening and the little that remained of the sun was a blood-red streak low in the clouds.

Alan was travelling to Cardiff to work on a long audit for the

firm of accountants which employed him. He didn't like the idea
of leaving London and his friends, but at least it would make
something of a change.

About an hour and a half out of Paddington the man folded
his paper and looked at his watch, which he drew from the
pocket of his waistcoat. He seemed agitated.

'I make it four-ten,' the man said. 'Is that what you make it?'

Alan looked at his own watch. 'Four-nine,' he said.

'Damnation,' the man said. 'I'm sure you're slow.'

'This is a new watch,' said Alan.

'Well, it's important that we get the right time. I must tell
you, I feel most uncomfortable travelling on this train, because
last night I dreamed that it was going to crash at precisely
twenty minutes past four.'

'Crash?' Alan felt nervous and laughed. 'Dreams don't come
true.'

'Oh, but they do,' said the man gloomily. 'I could see the
twisted metal and hear the sounds of people screaming.
Damned odd. It makes me feel terrible. It puts me in a bit of a
sweat.'

'I shouldn't worry about it,' Alan said.

'Worry about it? It terrifies me.' The man began to fidget
with his bag, doing and undoing the metal clip. 'Look here, I
never remember any of the dreams that I have. But why should
I remember this one?' Suddenly, he stood up, and paced quickly
to and fro.

In spite of himself Alan looked at his watch. He made it
twelve minutes past four. He looked out of the window, but
was very much aware of the way the elderly man was nervously
moving about. When he looked up at the man, Alan saw that
sweat drops were running down his face and that he was
chewing hard on his lower lip.

'Dreams don't mean a thing,' Alan said. 'You should ignore
it.' Just then, a woman in a brown hat walked past down the
corridor, and peered in through the window.

'I'm not sure about that,' said the man. 'I feel in a terrible
state. The truth is, I dreamed that I got killed in the crash.
Suppose there was a crash? Suppose this train did crash and I
got killed? Well, can I take that chance?' He anxiously opened
his bag.

Alan looked first at the woman, and then at his watch. All this was really rather silly, he felt. It was eighteen minutes past four. The woman in the corridor walked away, shaking her head.

He felt nervous himself, which was ridiculous.

The man looked at his own watch and then stood up again, lifting his black bag.

'What are you going to do?' Alan asked.

Without a word, the man threw open the train door and stepped out into the rushing air. The train, at the time, was travelling at sixty miles an hour. Alan jumped from his seat and, frightened and bewildered, not knowing quite how to behave, pulled hard on the communication cord. With a screeching of metal, the train rapidly came to a halt.

In a daze, Alan sat down. When the guard and ticket inspector came into the compartment, he said, 'There's a man on the line. He stood up and stepped out, right in front of my eyes!'

The railway officials looked both surprised and angry and a few other passengers, curious to know what was going on, crowded together in the corridor. Alan saw the woman in the brown hat pointing and talking.

The inspector, the guard, and the driver walked back down the line for about a mile. They found no one. Alan swore that a man had been in the compartment, and pointed to the newspaper on the seat opposite.

'He left that behind, if you don't believe me.'

The driver, annoyed at being behind schedule, picked the paper up.

'What's this supposed to prove?' he asked.

They looked at the paper. It was several years old and carried a front page story about a Paddington–Cardiff train that had crashed into a level crossing killing thirty-nine passengers.

Alan stared at the paper. There was a photograph of the same man who had been in the compartment and who had stepped out of the train. 'That's the man,' he said.

One of the inspectors pushed his cap back and scratched his head.

'I don't see how it could be,' he said. He read from the article. 'Amongst those killed was the prominent pathologist, Dr Michael Aitchinson (pictured above).'

Alan sat down, dazed. The driver, the guard, the ticket inspector, and the woman in the brown hat looked at him severely.

'There's a fine of twenty-five pounds for pulling the cord without good reason,' the guard remarked.

S.Q.

ADÈLE GERAS

This is a story with a moral. If you've got the same problem my sister had when she was a little girl, it may help you, or cheer you up. At least you'll have the comfort of knowing that someone else has been through it all before you.

In America they have this saying, which sounds funny but which makes sense. 'If life hands you lemons,' they say, 'make lemonade.' In other words, make the best of what happens to you in life. My sister has certainly done that.

Stephanie is three years younger than I am. When I was eight, she was five, and that was the first time we really noticed her problem, because by then she could tell us all about it, but I think, looking back, that she'd been troubled by nightmares since . . . well, since before she could talk properly.

Everyone has bad dreams from time to time. Sometimes we're anxious about things, and nightmares are just our brains working out our worries in picture form. Or perhaps we see something on TV or read something that terrifies us, and then we dream about it at night. That's the reason lots of parents, seeing their little ones clutching books which have skeletons or ghosts on the cover, come out with remarks like:

'You don't want to read that before bed. It'll give you nightmares.'

Steph was always a screamer. A few minutes after she fell asleep, she'd wake up again, and then the whole family sprang into action to try and get her to drop off once more. In the end, the lullaby or the hot drink or me sitting next to her cot and holding her fingers through the bars worked, and her eyes closed at last.

'Maybe tonight'll be different,' Mum used to say every day, but it never was.

Later on, when Steph knew how to say a few words, we'd ask her what was the matter when she woke up shrieking every night, but what she said made no sense at all.

'See flowers!' she'd scream. Or sometimes: 'Bad wall! Bad wall!' Once she cried: 'Go away, nasty stones. Don't want stones . . . make gone, make gone.' That was her way of saying: take them away.

Mum and Dad and I used to discuss Steph's strange nighttime behaviour. I felt quite grown-up, being allowed to stay up for supper after she'd been put to bed. We usually managed to get at least a bit of food down us before she woke up howling. I was the one who guessed what was wrong with her.

'I've got bad dreams,' I said. 'Stephie have bad dreams too.' (I was only four.)

'How can she?' my mum said. 'She has nothing but good, happy things all around her. You haven't been showing her anything scary, have you, Peter?'

I shook my head.

'She says "flowers" and once she said "ducks."'

'And had we been to feed the ducks that day?'

I nodded. 'But she liked ducks. She chased them.'

'Well,' said Dad in the voice of someone who knows what he's talking about, 'no one can possibly be having nightmares about flowers and clouds and walls and ducks. She's probably teething. Pass the mustard, Peter.'

She was, though. As she grew older, she told me a little about it.

'I hate going to sleep,' she said to me once. 'I see things.'

'Ghosty things? Scary things?'

She shook her head. 'Not really. Just normal things. But they scare me.'

'Tell me about what you see.'

But she wouldn't. She just shook her head.

By the time she started going to school, the waking-up in the night had become more and more common, only nowadays she had more sense than to shriek and scream and carry on and bring Mum and Dad running. She just woke up, and then came into my room, and woke me up, and I was the one who had to go back to her room with her and talk to her about other stuff till she fell asleep.

One day, Miss Harris, her teacher, stopped me in the corridor.

'Will you come and see me at dinner-time, Peter? I'm going to have a word with Stephanie, and I'd like you to be there.'

So there we were, me and Steph, sitting at one of the tables in Miss Harris's room, while all our friends played on the field outside the window.

'Stephanie tells me,' Miss Harris said, 'that the reason she looks so tired every day is because she has nightmares nearly every night.'

'She's always had them,' I said. 'Ever since she was a baby.'

Steph said nothing. She was busy scribbling on a piece of paper in front of her.

'I've told her she must tell someone about them,' said Miss Harris. 'And she's chosen you. I've told her that the best way to stop the nightmares is to write them down, exactly as though they were stories . . . and, of course, she can't write yet, so I'm afraid that you'll have to write them down for her for the next couple of years. Do you think you can do that, Peter?'

'Yes, Miss,' I said. 'I don't mind. I like story-writing.'

That was how it started. Every day, after school, I sat down at the kitchen table with Steph next to me on her special chair, and she'd start telling me her dreams. Every so often, I'd have to stop her and say:

'A little slower, Steph . . . I can't write as quickly as that. Say that bit again.'

They all came out then, years and years of dreams. Flowers that grew and grew and sucked you into them till you couldn't breathe: walls with a trellis wallpaper that had hideous grinning faces peeping out from it, and each face with eyes like fire that followed you wherever you went; stones that melted and lost their shape so that the landscape shifted and became dark and unknowable; clouds that massed over your head and stopped you from seeing where you were going; trees that plucked at your shoulders as you passed under them ... the list was endless.

After a few months of this, Steph had a whole exercise book full of these dreams.

'Your stable full of nightmares,' Miss Harris smiled. 'You should now try and see if you can dream about some pleasant things ... and call them your dayhorses!' (This was Miss Harris's idea of a joke.)

As soon as she could, she started to write them down herself, and I stopped thinking about them. They happened less frequently, for one thing. Steph stopped having so many nightmares *after* she began reading horror stories and ghost stories and anything scary should could get her hands on. This is not the way things usually work. Usually, scary stories *produce* bad dreams, but they seem to comfort my sister. She tried to explain it.

'If the scary thing is happening there, in the book, then it isn't happening to me. It makes me feel safe, in a funny kind of way. *My* nightmares . . .' she stopped.

'Go on,' I said. 'What about your nightmares?'

'It's ordinary things,' she said. 'I just see the scary side of ordinary things. Like forks, and windows, and light switches, and Hoovers . . . they make me nervous.'

We grew up, and gradually I stopped asking Steph about her dreams. She said nothing about them either, so I thought she maybe didn't have them any more. But one day, I was in her room when she opened the bottom drawer of her desk, and there they were: dozens and dozens of notebooks.

'What're all those?' I asked. 'There must be at least twenty notebooks there.'

'Thirty-six,' Steph said. 'Full ones. And a couple still to be written in.'

'Whatever's in them?'

'My dreams.'

'I don't believe it . . . are you still writing them down, like Miss Harris from Primary School told you to?'

'Yes,' she said. 'And one day they're going to come in handy. Wait and see.'

And they did. Nowadays, if you go into any railway station or airport, you'll see books with two gold initials shining out from a black cover: S.Q., it'll say. And then the title in smaller gold letters. Something like: *The Terror of Tulips*, or *Behind the Mask* or *The Moving Wallpaper*. Stephanie's novels. She's the best-selling horror novelist in the country. Her sales are approaching those of her hero, Stephen King. That accounts for the initials. They're a kind of joke. When she had her first book published, she said:

'There's a Stephen King, so I'll be a Stephanie Queen.'

That became S.Q. which is better because it's more mysterious . . . no one knows quite who the author is. Is it a woman or a man? The publishers guard her secret closely.

And the moral? Use what you have. Make the best of it. If life hands you horrors, every single night, then turn them into horror stories.

Uncle Walter

JOHN GORDON

manda always enjoyed staying with Uncle Walter because his stories were so horrible. Aunt Jessy thought they were so deeply upsetting that she forbade him to frighten Amanda with his awful tales, which was why Amanda was always hoping to get him on his own without Aunt Jessy being there to spoil things.

One night, it was in the middle of her holiday and she was staying up later than she ever did at home, she had the perfect opportunity. Supper was over, the oil lamp had been turned down so that, from outside, the cottage was shutting its eyes and settling down to slumber through the long night huddled in its lonely corner of the dark fields. Aunt Jessy was busy with some late task somewhere in the back of the house, leaving Amanda and Uncle Walter sitting together in the firelight. For a minute or more they watched the flames flapping at the logs

without a sound, and then Uncle Walter took out his pocket
knife and began to peel an apple.

'You get used to it,' he said.

'You mean the quietness?' said Amanda because that was
what was on her mind. The darkness outside had heaped silence
right up to the doorstep.

'There's that,' he threw a long snake of apple peel on to the
fire, 'and other things.'

Now Amanda was in hopes of a story. 'What other things?'
she said.

'This and that,' he said. 'You know what I mean.'

'No, I don't.' Many people thought Amanda quite a pretty
girl, but sometimes found her a bit too sharp 'for her own good'.
She didn't care.

Her uncle was not put out by her quick words. He slid a slice
of apple from his blade into his mouth, chewed for a juicy
moment, then said, 'I was thinking of the war—we even got
used to that, at the time.' He paused. 'Things happened in the
war you would hardly credit.'

Amanda was about to say that she knew that, too, but he
waved the knife-holding hand to prevent her interrupting.
'People did things in the war, really horrible things, even out
here.'

Amanda doubted it. 'Mum told me it was so peaceful here
you had children staying with you to get away from the
bombing.'

He nodded. 'Evacuees,' he said.

'She always said they were safe here.'

'She did, did she?' Uncle Walter smiled and his plump cheeks
glistened like red fruit resting in the husk of his short beard.
'Well, she don't know everything, your mother.'

Amanda waited, but he sat quite still, leaning forward slightly
so that the flames threw the shadow of his broad shoulders
upwards to stretch like dark wings from side to side of the ceiling.

'The evacuees never did anyone any harm,' said Amanda,
hoping to encourage him.

'That's true,' he said. 'That's very, very true. But that isn't to
say they got away without harm being done to *them*.' He
paused again, maddeningly, before he went on. 'They weren't
the only ones staying here at that time, don't forget.'

'How can I forget something I never knew? I wasn't here, was I?'

The exasperation in her voice made him turn towards her. He was not a tall man but he was very strongly built and to see all that bulk swinging around to face her merely because of the tone in her voice made Amanda fall silent. She was not sure what she had started.

His eyes were as large and black as an owl's, and they rested on her before he spoke. 'When the war was on,' he said softly, 'it wasn't only evacuees we had in the village; we had soldiers.'

Soldiers. It was the way he drew out the word, making the esses hiss like the apple peel on the fire, that made Amanda shudder. That, and Uncle Walter's huge eyes that seemed to expect her to know more about soldiers than she did.

'They weren't all nice, brave young men,' he said, and turned away as if that was the end of the matter.

Amanda could not let it rest there. She fidgeted in her chair.

'You sound like a kitten in a basket,' said Uncle Walter, and Amanda gave a tiny miaow. 'And you needn't think you are going to get round me like that, young lady. I'm not in the mood to stroke kittens.'

Oh yes, you are, thought Amanda, and in a small, pleading voice she said, 'What did the soldiers do, Uncle Walter? I won't be able to go to sleep if you don't tell me.'

At that he put out one of his big hands as if she really was a kitten and he was about to pluck her out of her chair. She caught one glimpse of the large, hairy paw coming towards her and could not prevent herself shrinking down into her cushions. He smiled when he saw he had made her anxious, and said, 'Just you be careful, my girl, or you'll be in as much trouble as I'll get into if I say any more.'

'I shan't tell on you, Uncle Walter.' The words had come out too quickly and when he suddenly opened his mouth wide she was afraid she had annoyed him. The sight of his large white teeth made her stiffen, but then he raised the apple to his mouth and took a bite.

For a moment his jaws crunched and he stared into the flames as though he was making up his mind about something. Then he swallowed, turned the apple in his hands, and with his knife cut a slice from the unbitten side.

'You'll be the death of me,' he said, 'but I reckon I've gone so far I can't turn back now.'

He held the slice of apple to the blade with his thumb and offered it to her. Amanda did not want to take it, but he jerked it towards her and said, 'Go on, have it. We're in this thing together.' It was very slippery in her fingers.

'It was when them soldiers was here,' he said. 'A young evacuee girl went missing, and she wasn't ever found.'

'Not ever?' said Amanda.

'Never. Some said she'd run away because she was homesick, but no one believed it.' He looked at her, and even though it was the last thing she wanted to do at that moment she felt she had to put the apple in her mouth. 'And don't you ever tell your Aunt Jessy that I told you this. She don't like to be reminded.'

Amanda swallowed the apple and shook her head. 'I won't.'

'It was one of them soldiers took her. We all knew that, but that didn't make any difference. The police came around asking questions of all us village boys and never takin' no for an answer when we said we never knew a thing about it. They gave us such a bad time that we began to wonder if it wasn't one of us after all. It was a terrible feeling, Amanda—being suspected about something you haven't done. They even searched the houses.'

'This one?' Amanda's voice was very small, and in the warm room a thin, cold draught coiled itself around her arms and legs.

'This one . . . and the old barn down the lane.'

Amanda knew the barn. It was two fields away along an overgrown track that was never used, and she had made herself a secret corner in it that no one knew about, except perhaps Uncle Walter, who seemed to know most things she did.

'That old barn would have been just the place where she might have been taken, but there wasn't a thing there. That girl was far away and gone for good, and everyone could have told them that—especially one of them soldiers. But the whole world had turned upside down until you began to wonder if somehow or other, like in a horrible nightmare, you might have done something while you was asleep. That might seem daft, but that's how you got to thinking.'

He stopped talking and sat silent, hunched in front of the fire.

'Didn't they ever find out who it was?' Amanda spoke so

quietly she wondered if he had heard, but suddenly he split the apple in half with his knife and threw the pieces among the burning logs.

'Of course they didn't!' He snapped his clasp knife shut. 'Why do you think I still have dreams about it?' He gave a snort and got to his feet, his big eyes glaring, even his teeth glinting in the firelight, and she could not prevent herself shrinking deeper into her chair.

But then he saw her, and his hairy fists unclenched and he was Uncle Walter once more, smiling as he looked down on her. 'Oh, my goodness,' he said, 'when you look scared like that your mouth's no bigger than a button.'

'I can't help it.'

'You don't have to. It just makes you look like a little doll, that's all—and I should never have told you all that stuff.'

Aunt Jessy's voice came from the doorway. 'All what stuff?' Neither of them had heard the door open, and now she came in and stood looking at them both. 'Walter,' she said sternly, 'you haven't been telling her one of your terrible tales again, have you?' She moved her sharp eyes from one to the other and made up her mind. 'Yes you have, you wicked man! I can tell from the poor child's expression that she's scared half out of her wits.'

Uncle Walter began to say something, but when Aunt Jessy was in a mood like this she did not give him a chance. All he could do was wink at Amanda from behind Aunt Jessy's back before he was sent bustling into the kitchen to make cocoa for 'the poor child' to help her sleep.

For once, Amanda was glad to go to bed and escape from Uncle Walter and his tales. She sank into the big feather bed until it made a nest around her, and when Aunt Jessy had tucked her in she left a candle burning in Amanda's room 'for company'. But bed was not as restful as it should have been. Amanda was aware of the huge night lying on the fields where foxes barked under the stars and hedgehogs snuffled in the grass, and she lay awake in the candlelight unable to close her eyes until she heard Aunt Jessy and Uncle Walter coming upstairs and settling down in the room next to hers.

She closed her eyes, and tiredness came sliding down until it covered her and she slept. She began to dream. It was the strange dream she had from time to time. It was the dream in which she knew she was asleep, and she also knew she was dreaming. She was asleep, but she could see herself lying in bed so clearly that she was certain she could make herself sit up. But the other thing she knew was that no matter how she strained her muscles she would never be able to stir even a finger.

She tried to sit up now, putting all her effort into it and, for the first time ever, she seemed to move. The candle had guttered in its candlestick and gone out, and in the darkness she was not sure whether her eyes were open or shut. It did not trouble her because she knew it was a dream, and in her sleep she willed a leg to move. She felt her toes push clear of the eiderdown and she sighed. This time, unlike in the other dreams, she could move.

In her dream she lowered both feet to the floor, felt the rug beneath her and stepped forward. The bare boards were cool enough to make her toes curl, but then she was at the door and stepping out on to the landing.

Her dream made everything larger. Now the cramped landing was huge, and strange shadows startled her. From somewhere in the darkness came the slow rise and fall of her uncle's breathing. The sound echoed around her, hollowed itself like a sea wave drawing back before it humped its shoulders and frothed and hissed forward until it seemed to snatch at her ankles and chill her legs, and before it could reach higher she found herself running ahead of it. Uncle Walter had become a creature that walked in the night.

She was at a door. It opened, but a new sound made her twist her head to look back. The footsteps told her that Uncle Walter was walking towards her, gazing through the darkness with his owl eyes. She struggled to get through the doorway as his padded footfalls came nearer, but her sleeve had caught on the door handle. She tore at it until with a last desperate wrench her sleeve came away in tatters and her arm felt the cold night air.

She was running. The ground was rough and cut her bare feet. She stumbled, crouched and listened. He was there, somewhere in the darkness, listening. She crawled, but panic made her heart thump and then she was running once more, but now thick grass clogged her feet and she was forcing herself through bushes that dragged at her arms and made her shut her eyes against the whips of thin branches.

She staggered. Somewhere there was a voice crying her name. It terrified her. She was crawling forward. The voice was her uncle's, filling the night, and she had to get away from it. But now a dark building loomed above her, and a huge door. Her hands touched it and she raised herself by pushing against it, but as she did so it seemed to float away from her and she moved into deeper darkness than the night itself.

In her dream the air was stuffy. She tried to wake herself, to will herself back into bed, but nothing obeyed her. She could hardly breathe, but even in her fear she knew by the smell of the air that she had been here before. She knew, and in that moment she woke.

The dream fell away, but she was no longer in her bed, nor even in her room. The cool, lavender smell of her bedroom had vanished, and in its place the air was full of the mustiness of dry, dusty boards and ancient sacking. She recognized it, but her brain refused to believe it.

She was huddled in a corner, struggling to put all the fragments together in her feverish mind when tall, thin streaks of light wavered and danced in the darkness ahead of her. They jumped and changed, fading and brightening until a single flash threw enough light to show her the angles and corners of the space that surrounded her. And the smell made her certain. She was far from the cottage, crouching on an earth floor and hugging her knees in the old barn. The light came through the cracks in the wooden walls. It moved and she watched it until it reached the door which she herself had pushed open. A pale, ghostly figure stood there. Its white gown reached the floor, and its arms were stretched towards her.

Amanda cried out. The air was sucked into her lungs to shriek again when the figure spoke to her. The voice was soft. 'There, there, my pet,' it said. 'There's nothing to be afraid of. This is just me,' and as the figure came closer she saw Aunt Jessy's face . . . Aunt Jessy in her night gown standing in the beam of a torch held in the hand of Uncle Walter.

Aunt Jessy held her close, and Amanda clung to her and whispered, 'What happened? Why am I not in bed?'

'You went sleepwalking, my lovely. Uncle Walter heard you going down the stairs, but by the time we got out of bed you were outside and we'd lost you.'

'But not for long,' said Uncle Walter. 'I caught a glimpse of you flitting along the path, and I guessed where you were heading.'

'Oh you did, did you?' Aunt Jessy was not pleased with him. 'And I can guess why you had such a good idea where she was. It's because you've been filling her head with your horrible stories . . . you ought to be ashamed of yourself.'

Laughter rumbled in Uncle Walter's chest, but Amanda hid her face in Aunt Jessy's shoulder so that she would not see his white teeth.

Dream Fountain

DENNIS HAMLEY

Carola knows she is in the capital of Transylvania.

She stirs and sits up in a four-poster bed. She hears birdsong and hears church bells ringing. Sunlight pours through huge windows.

The door opens. A man comes in. Black trousers, shiny waistcoat. Round face with pointy nose. Black hair, shiny as his waistcoat, plastered flat to his head.

He places a tray by her bed and leaves. Walking backwards, bowing as he goes.

Carola is a princess in Transylvania. She has been given a princess's breakfast.

Carola drinks a wonderfully tasting juice from a goblet of pure crystal. She eats toast from a china plate so fine she can nearly see through it. A little silver spoon waits for her with which to eat her egg, which is so white that she thinks of other days when the world is covered in purest snow.

Carola combs out her long hair, fine as webs of royal spiders, golden as corn in sunlit fields. She puts on a dress, blue like a clear sky, edged with finest lace, which reaches to the floor.

Servants sigh with pleasure and clap hands in delight as she floats with such grace down a long, curved staircase. Huge double doors open for her. Now she stands in a bustling street. Tall, old buildings with windows like blank eyes cast shadows across pavements and tramtracks. Church bells still ring.

Another bell sounds, jangling and harsh. A yellow tram sidles up and stops. She boards it. She sits behind the driver. He has a bald patch on the back of his head. Shiny black hair is plastered to his skull on both sides like the wings of an oily bird. The tram slithers round bends like a metal snake. When Carola steps off she sees the driver has a round face with a pointy nose.

Carola stands alone on soft springy grass in a garden. The tall buildings are gone. Wooded hills surround her. On top of the hills are castles and towers, some ruined. A bird perches on her shoulder but when she reaches to touch it, it is gone.

The bells, too, are gone. Now there is a faint rushing sound. Carola follows it. Her heart sinks. She does not know why.

She walks through the garden under high archways. The first arch is twined with honeysuckle. Strange plants twist round the second. The rushing noise is louder. Carola goes under a third arch, made of stone, old and worn, covered with green mosses and golden brown lichens.

Now the rushing has become a roar which fills her head. This is where she is supposed to be, in front of the towering fountain. It stands there, like a rocket waiting to go to the moon. Fear snatches at Carola's heart. She sees herself twisting through limitless, airless space for ever.

The fountain rears up on four huge, splayed feet set in the middle of a pool. Water curves from the top and falls down either side. There are four ledges round the column. The lowest is the widest: the top ledge is the smallest.

Water falling from above plays round each ledge. It spills over the sides to the ledge below. From the lowest ledge the water drops straight into the deep pool and sends spray into Carola's face.

The pool is guarded by sharp rocks. On these rocks are statues. They look at Carola. The statues are mermaids and mermen. Nothing can move them or fill them with fear. Carola wants to be like them. She is suddenly reckless.

She climbs onto the nearest rock. She sits next to a mermaid. More spray drenches her.

The mermaid's lips move as if she speaks to Carola. The other stone mermaids and mermen look at her and their lips move too. She cannot hear what they say. But she is sure *something* speaks to her.

Then she knows. *It is the fountain that speaks.* Carola must hear what it is telling her.

Now she is in the icy water. It sends shocks through her body.

She reaches the lowest ledge. Underneath the ledge it is dark. Spray blinds her. She grips the ledge with both hands. Now she is sitting on it. She leans against one of the splayed feet which hold the fountain up. A curtain of roaring water shuts her off from everything beyond.

The fountain's roar is not mere noise. There are differences in it, like voices in a choir. The water which falls from the very top on to the first ledge sounds tinkly, light and high, like a girl's voice. This is how a mermaid would sing if she could.

The next one down sounds lower, the third lower still, the torrent plunging from the bottom ledge falls into the pool with a deep bass. All together, they make a watery scale.

She listens again. In this scale there are voices. *The fountain is calling her.*

The tinkly voice trills: 'Do not trust us, Carola.'

The second voice cries: 'Carola, we are too strong for you.'

The third voice rumbles: 'Sometimes we are treacherous. That is the way with water. One minute your friend, the next your enemy.'

The voice from the bottom ledge, deep and loud, intones. 'Surely some dreadful danger is at hand.'

Carola listens. She should be afraid. But she is not. She loves the fountain. She knows it is her friend. It gives her good advice. She has been told a secret, though she does not know what it is.

Carola woke up in her room full of posters and books. She sat up, feeling slightly dazed. She has just been somewhere strange. No, it has gone. But it didn't matter. Today would be a good one.

A voice called up the stairs. 'Come on, Carola. You'll be late.'

She scrambled out of bed, into the bathroom, back to her bedroom, threw her clothes on and was soon downstairs eating breakfast.

'I've packed you a lunch,' said Mum. 'Enjoy the trip.'

Carola left the house. Her class was going on a field visit. She would be with her best friends, Chloe and Debby, Clive and Kenny. They lived in the same road and went to school together. The form teacher, Mrs Fereday, would call the register and then they would file out to the coach.

'Has everybody got a packed lunch?' Mrs Fereday asked. 'Have you got good, strong shoes? You'll be walking a lot. Has everybody something waterproof to wear? You can never be sure of the weather this time of year.'

The form's affirmative answers straggled out.

The coach waited. It was yellow. Everybody filed on board.

Carola sat next to Chloe. Clive and Kenny were behind them. Debby sat across the gangway. Mrs Fereday was talking to the driver. Then she turned to count the pupils. The driver turned with her.

He had a round face with a pointed nose. His shiny black hair was plastered down each side of his head. When he turned back and started the coach, Carola saw he had a bald patch at the back.

Carola was sure she had seen him somewhere before. As the coach set off out of town, Carola worried about where. The answer was just round a corner in her mind and she couldn't somehow look that far.

First, the coach passed shops and houses, then headed out into the country. Far away on the horizon were hills, like the faint mauve shoulders of giants. Nearer, they became darker, until they reached to the sky in many shades of green. The road wound along the floor of a deep valley. The hills were wooded and steep. Carola looked up, for castles and towers, some ruined, which she knew would line the tops.

There were none.

But there should be, she thought. *They're always there.* A strange, cold fear and doubt spread through her.

The narrow road zigzagged up a steep hill. Carola could see the driver, with his bald patch and black hair like a bird's folded wings, hunched over the steering wheel as the coach snaked round the bends. The diesel engine roared and shrieked as it strained up the hills. Everyone talked—all except Carola.

Above the diesel howl and babbling voices she thought she heard bells ringing. Yet there were no towers for them to ring from.

Chloe jabbed her with her elbow, making her jump. 'Cheer up, Carola. What's the matter? You haven't said a word since we left.'

They were near the end of their journey. Soon they were parked alongside other coaches. They had reached the Nature Reserve. Before they got off, Mrs Fereday stood up to talk to them.

'Right, we're here. First, the warden will tell us where to go and what to look for. Then we'll eat our lunches. And there's no excuse for not putting your rubbish away properly. Then we'll follow the nature trail. Everything is well signposted and there'll always be a teacher or one of the centre staff nearby, so there's no excuse for getting into trouble. The trail climbs away from here as far as the big waterfall, then it curves round and comes back here a different way. You're to stay in your small groups and you're *never* to leave the trail. And remember: we're always just behind you.'

First they went to a low building made of logs where the warden told them about the Reserve, and the wild-life—and especially about the high waterfall and the foaming stream beneath it. Carola listened and when she heard about the falls and the foam she shivered because of that fear which kept coming.

Then they went back to the coach and ate their lunches. Soon it was time to start the trail.

Carola, Chloe, Debby, Clive, and Kenny made up one group. They set off, following the waymarks, through dense woods, across bare, heathery moors, between tall, grey rocks. Sometimes they even watched out for what they had been told to.

Gradually came the sound of water, nearer and nearer, louder and louder: water roaring, falling from a great height, beating at her ears, filling her mind. Now she knew what she had been waiting for all morning. *The day would end with the roaring of water. The bus driver was there to warn her. Not seeing ruined towers lining the hills made the warning clearer.*

To shut this warning out she clapped her hands over her ears.

They climbed under trees until they reached the top. There were the falls in front of them. A bow of bright water cascaded down steep, stepped rocks into a pool which led into a foamily gurgling stream. Something icy gripped Carola's heart.

'Look at that,' said Clive.

'It's fantastic,' said Chloe.

'What's on top?' asked Kenny. 'Where does it come from?'

'You can't see,' said Debby. 'The trail only goes along the bottom.'

She pointed to a little wooden bridge across the pool.

'I could climb up and find where the stream on the top comes from,' said Clive.

'You'd never make it,' said Kenny.

'The warden said we mustn't leave the trail,' said Debby.

'She won't know,' said Clive. 'I'll be down before she notices.'

And then Carola found herself speaking. They weren't her words. Something was making her say them and it was very urgent that Clive should listen. '*Do not trust it, Clive.*'

'Rubbish,' said Clive. 'I can look after myself.'

'*Clive, it is treacherous. That is the way with water. One minute your friend, the next your enemy.*'

'Carola, why are you talking like that?' cried Chloe. 'Stop it. It's weird. I don't like it.'

But these words came from deep inside her and she couldn't stop them even though she wanted to.

'*Surely some dreadful danger is at hand,*' she shouted.

'Don't you worry about me,' Clive shouted back.

'You'll get drenched,' Debby called. 'You might fall.'

'Never,' was Clive's answer. 'Just watch me.'

'Perhaps he'll do it. You never know,' said Kenny.

'He'll get us all in trouble,' said Debby.

'He's an idiot. He'll get himself hurt,' said Chloe.

For a second he disappeared behind the falling water. Then Carola saw him climbing the rocks at the side, carefully and slowly.

'*Surely some dreadful . . .*' Carola started: then a clear memory of wading through water past cascading torrents came into her mind. And the memory made her act, because she knew she had to. Once she started, she would be told what to do. She didn't know how, but she knew she would. She started to follow Clive up the side of the waterfall.

She stepped into the freezing water. The roar deafened her. Flying spray drenched her. She started climbing slippery rocks. She scrabbled with hands and feet for safe holds and twice nearly fell.

Desperately, she looked upwards. Far away, she saw Clive's feet struggling for holds, sometimes slipping. She passed the first ledge. Clive's feet slipped worse than ever. If he fell, he'd take her with him. Her hands were numb with cold: she was wet through to the skin.

She should know by now what to do. She listened for the voices in the water which would give her hope. All she heard was the great rushing roar which nothing could stop. Then

Clive's feet disappeared. She gasped. Her stomach churned round. Had he lost his footing?

Sudden fear smothered her, strong enough to make her faint there and then. But what good would that do Clive?

He was still there. Carola made herself climb on, blindly but amazingly without ever losing her footing. She was close to the top now, where the water dropped over. She burst through the drenching and roaring and, with a last final heave over the top, she was there.

They had made it. She and Clive stood together, at the point where smooth water curved over and crashed downwards, to break up below them with awful force.

Together, they looked down. Chloe, Debby, Kenny, and others from their class looked up—as well as Mrs Fereday, looking worried, and the warden, looking furious.

Carola stared at them. Something strange happened. One minute all those faces came up close. She knew what Mrs Fereday was thinking—*how will we get them down? How will I tell the parents?* She saw the warden was talking into a mobile phone.

Yes, all those faces were close. The next instant, they were far, far away, as if on another planet. Then they were close again, then they were far off. To and fro, near and far they seemed to go before her eyes: near and far, to and fro. Everything she had feared was happening—*right now.*

She turned and looked at Clive. He looked back. He stumbled. She swayed with fright. They grabbed at each other's arms for support.

Then, suddenly—did they slip, did they struggle, *did the waterfall decide for them?*—they were falling, falling, and the waterfall kept up its wordless roar as they tumbled helplessly past . . .

Carola sits up in her four-poster bed in the capital of Transylvania. She is brought her breakfast. When she has eaten it she combs out her hair and puts on her lovely sky-blue dress.

When she gets off the tram and comes to the gardens, she will visit her good friend the fountain. The last time she was there, she remembers, the fountain told her something very important. She cannot remember what it was.

As the water's roar grows louder, she tries hard to remember. And when she sees mermaids and mermen, this time they are smiling, as if they expect her and welcome her. When she is near the rocks and the shining foam and the fountain towers over her, she thinks—*I do not know what the fountain told me. But I do know that it was right.*

Perhaps she might climb higher this time, right up the fountain's ledges, maybe up to the very top . . .

No, she mustn't. A voice in her head says to her, 'Don't listen. Don't listen to the fountain, Carola.'

She hears voices.

'*Do not trust us.*'

'Don't listen. Don't listen.'

There's another voice, outside her this time, coming from far away. 'Is she all right?'

'*Treacherous. We are treacherous.*'

Another voice from outside her, alarmed and urgent: 'I don't know. I can't tell. We must get her back.'

Cold. Carola is very cold. And wet.

But she is a princess here in Transylvania.

Frisky

KENNETH IRELAND

The cat was quite small, black and white, and scratching at the kitchen door at the time. It was obviously a stray from somewhere. When Mrs Mason opened the door it mewed piteously.

'Poor thing!' said Mrs Mason.

When her daughter, Juliet, went to look as well, however, she decided there was something distinctly strange about this cat. And it wasn't only because it had scratched at the door in the first place as if it belonged there.

As soon as she got to the door it stood perfectly still and stared at her and its eyes narrowed. It seemed to be examining her thoughtfully. Then its tail began to twitch.

'The poor thing must be hungry. Bring a saucer of milk for it,' said her mother.

Obediently Juliet did as she was told, and the cat's tail waved as she bent down to put the saucer on the ground. They watched it lap the milk. What Juliet noticed especially was that while most cats would concentrate only on the milk, this one kept its eyes on her all the time. That, she decided, was even stranger.

Then it sat, watching the two of them, licking its lips, its tail still swaying from side to side. Then it got up and frisked around a little, playfully, before settling down again.

'I think we might adopt it,' said her mother, 'as a pet.'

Juliet was not so sure. 'It probably belongs to somebody,' she said doubtfully.

She particularly didn't like the way the cat kept looking at her so unnervingly. But then it rose to its feet, climbed daintily over the doorstep and started rubbing itself against her legs, purring softly as it weaved in and out.

'See, he likes you,' declared her mother brightly and encouragingly.

What Juliet noticed now was that the cat looked at her mother as soon as she said this, almost as if it understood what she was saying.

'I'm not so sure that I like it at all,' said Juliet. 'Somehow there's something—'

The cat leapt outside the door again, and started frisking around in front of them a second time, before abruptly returning to weave itself in and out of her legs.

'You know you've always wanted a pet,' said her mother, convinced. 'So now you've got one. We'll call it Frisky.'

'But I didn't want a cat,' retorted Juliet.

Particularly not this one. She didn't like the way Frisky kept looking at her, in a way which if the creature had been human would have almost been sneering. She was surprised her mother couldn't see the look on its face. There was something different, something very unusual about it, she was convinced of that.

But while she was still struggling to put into words what she felt was wrong with it, the cat casually strolled past the two of them and inside the house. And when they found it next, it was sitting on the window ledge in the front room looking out as if it really belonged.

As soon as they entered the room it leapt down, frisked about playfully then began to rub itself against Juliet's legs again.

'I think,' said her mother, smiling, 'that settles it, don't you?'

The trouble began almost at once. When her father returned home he obviously approved as well. He bent down and stroked it, and it purred encouragingly.

That cat, decided Juliet, knew on which side its bread was buttered, almost as if it had planned deliberately to stay from the beginning. And when later they were all sitting down to watch television the cat leapt on to his knee then lay there, again purring. Her father stroked it again, idly, while Frisky looked up innocently into his face.

Then it jumped down from there and lay on her mother's knee instead, then after a short while took a leap on to Juliet's.

'See?' remarked her mother. 'It's made itself at home. We can't possibly turn it out now.'

Just what this thing intended all along, thought Juliet. Then she realized. She was already assuming this cat possessed human thoughts, was capable of human reasoning. And that was impossible, or ought to be.

'Ow!' she exclaimed suddenly.

Frisky had dug all its claws into both her legs simultaneously, like little daggers going into her flesh.

'He didn't mean it,' said her mother sympathetically. 'He just doesn't know any better. Frisky was only trying to make himself comfortable.'

The cat jumped down to the carpet, where it sat, regarding her cunningly, as Juliet stood up.

'It knew exactly what it was doing,' said Juliet, rubbing her thighs. 'It did it on purpose.'

'Don't be silly, Juliet, of course it didn't. Cats just can't help doing that sort of thing sometimes. It was an accident, that's all.'

When Juliet, still not convinced, went to the bathroom to inspect the damage, she saw the little specks of blood the cat had drawn, and had to open the medicine cabinet to find the antiseptic to dab on the wounds.

Cats, she knew, did sometimes dig their claws in when they sat on people's knees. But not so deliberately nor usually so viciously that they actually fetched blood.

This cat had known exactly what it was doing, she had no doubt about that now. Even more alarming, she was almost certain now that this particular cat had actually planned to be invited into their house, and had intended to injure her for some reason known only to itself.

It grew worse. Always, but only when either her mother or father was about, it would rub itself purring against her legs, just as the first time they had seen it at their door. And as long as either of them remained near, that was all it would do.

But as soon as they had left, a vicious set of claws would appear and the cat would swipe her almost casually across her legs. Or even, on some occasions, there would not be its claws, but the cat would actually sink its teeth into her before wandering off to sit somewhere else in the room.

Then when her parents would return, curious, after her shout, the picture they would see would be the happy domestic scene of a docile Frisky sitting in a corner cleaning its fur placidly—and Juliet rubbing the most recent damage which had been inflicted.

Why couldn't her parents see what was really happening? Why wouldn't they believe her each time she told them the truth? Each time, at first, they had merely sympathized, but very soon that turned into accusing her of actually tormenting Frisky to make him do such a thing.

'It only happens when we're out of the room,' said her mother, 'so it can only be that you're doing something to poor Frisky while we're not there, doesn't it?'

'I don't do anything to him,' complained Juliet. 'It's just that whenever you're out of the room he attacks me, without warning and for no reason.'

'You're making that up,' said her mother firmly. 'Like when you said he always bites you whenever you put his food down for him.'

'But he does!' Juliet burst out.

'So you say. Now let me watch while you do it.'

They were in the kitchen at the time. She filled Frisky's bowl, since it was time for his meal, then handed it to Juliet.

'Now you just put that down on the floor for him and let's see what happens, shall we?'

Hesitantly, Juliet took the bowl from her mother and gingerly bent down to put it on the floor. Frisky, dancing about eagerly as soon as he saw the bowl, as he always did, at once began to eat, waving his tail in delight as he did.

Juliet stood up, relieved that she had not been bitten this time, but still perplexed.

'There you are, no problem at all, was there?' asked her mother brightly.

Juliet remained behind regarding Frisky thoughtfully after her mother left the kitchen. No, there had been no problem at all that time, her mother had been quite right about that. Now the cat had finished and sat preening itself, she decided to put the bowl into the sink ready for washing-up. As soon as she reached down for it, without any warning of what he intended to do, Frisky promptly sank his teeth into her fingers.

Juliet yelled in pain.

Her mother came back at once. 'Now what did you do to him?' she demanded.

'Nothing. He just waited until you'd gone out, as always,' said Juliet crossly.

'I think,' said her mother carefully, 'that you'd better leave him alone until you've decided to admit to what you keep doing to him, young lady. I'd never have expected you to be jealous of a cat! And that's the real truth of the matter, isn't it?'

No use trying to explain that wasn't the truth at all, but almost certainly the direct opposite of what her mother believed. She almost convinced herself that Frisky was actually smiling secretly at her as she left the kitchen. Except, of course, ordinary cats can't do that.

The decision came later when Juliet was out in the garden to find Frisky sitting next to a tall pile of bricks which had just been delivered. Her father intended to rebuild the old wall at the end of the garden, when he got round to it. In the meantime the bricks lay where the builder's merchant had placed them.

Juliet looked round. Nobody to hear her. Frisky sat looking up at her, far too intelligently for any ordinary cat, she decided.

'So where did you really come from?' Juliet found herself asking it. 'And why did you come to our house?'

She made sure she kept a safe distance between the two of them. Best not to bend down while she was talking to this creature, or it might jump on her face.

'You know exactly what I'm saying, don't you?' she added, surprising herself.

Frisky looked modestly at his front paws, then back up at

her again. It seemed that he really did understand, then. Then Frisky opened his mouth to form a broad, almost human, grin and stared into Juliet's face mockingly.

'You keep away from me,' said Juliet fiercely.

Trembling, she went to stand round the other side of the pile of new bricks while she thought the matter out more carefully. When she leaned against it, the pile moved, just slightly. The evil cat was sitting directly behind it.

Juliet suddenly heaved with all her might, and the pile, almost as tall as herself, fell with a crash. Juliet scrambled over it and jumped all over the fallen bricks. She could see one small, dark-furred leg sticking out, still moving. Then that stopped. Panting, she began to re-erect the bricks into their original pile.

She buried the crushed body, using a spade from the tool shed, in an empty patch of ground at the end of the garden, stamping it down firmly. That would settle that, she decided.

Her parents were surprised that Frisky was missing, and her mother spent some time wandering round the garden calling 'Frisky! Frisky!' Juliet thought it best not to offer any explanation. Let them think what they liked, it was unlikely they would ever find the body.

'Perhaps he'll come back tomorrow, or even later tonight,' said her mother confidently. 'Cats are like that, you know.'

Not this one, not now, thought Juliet grimly.

She was in bed when she thought she heard a mewing sound outside her bedroom door. Ever since Frisky had arrived she had made sure her bedroom door was closed firmly at night, to make sure it couldn't come in while she was asleep and helpless.

Now she climbed out of bed, went to the door and opened it just a fraction, but not wide enough even for a cat to creep through. There was no way it could have been Frisky, of course, but she still had to check.

Nothing was there. It must have been her imagination. She switched on the light to make sure. Then she went back to bed.

Next she heard the same sound at the window, followed by a faint scratching. She had been asleep at the time, but at once was wide awake again. The window had been shut tight as well. Cats, she knew, could climb. She didn't want one evening to find Frisky trying to get in through there to her—when he had been alive, that was.

She slowly drew back the curtain. Again, nothing, certainly no cat outside on the window ledge trying to get in. Not that she had expected to find a cat rather like Frisky out there, of course. She even opened the window wide and peered out. She was safe. She went back to bed, first closing the window firmly again.

It was in the middle of the night that she heard not a mewing but a hissing and spitting, like an angry cat—inside the bedroom and very close to her. In a panic she stretched up her hand to switch on the light, and to her horror saw sitting on the end of her bed, his tail waving from side to side—Frisky!

Her parents, hearing her anguished cries a few moments later, rushed into her bedroom.

'It was a nightmare!' gasped Juliet. 'I thought it was Frisky!'

Then she saw the ripped bedclothes, blood on the sheets, and could feel the deep scratches on her face, neck, and arms.

'So now we know, don't we?' remarked her mother ominously. 'You've always wanted to get rid of that poor cat, don't think I haven't noticed. And now even though he's not here you're still pretending. Isn't that rather silly? Nightmare, indeed! All the

time you've been making these scratches yourself, haven't you? What have you been using—your nail file?'

'But it really was—' began Juliet. 'He nearly killed me . . .'

Her parents looked round the bedroom. The window was shut. The door had been firmly closed before they had opened it themselves to come in.

'Are you trying to tell us,' said her father grimly, 'that Frisky got in here? That's quite impossible, and you know it. Or are you trying to pretend it was some sort of ghost instead? If this goes on, you might have to see a doctor, before you do yourself some real harm.'

It was no use trying to explain any more. After her wounds had been washed and the antiseptic dabbed on, and her parents had returned to their own room, Juliet lay trembling in bed. She knew what was going to happen now.

The next time she shouted in fear and pain, her parents would take no notice.

She was right. They didn't.

The White-washed Room

GERALD KERSH

She was one of those hearty, healthy young women whom you may see every day in towns like Guildford. You see them and you hear them. They wear good tweed execrably cut and, more often than not, are accompanied by pink-faced men in yellow turtle-necked sweaters and big flannel trousers, who wear—as it were with an air of astonishment—brushed-up gingerish moustaches. The men with the moustaches stand condescendingly filling foul old briar pipes, or lighting cigarettes, while conversing at the tops of their voices—usually with one big, booted foot on the running-board of a small, fast, yet dilapidated little car.

She came of an excellent family. She could out-ride, out-smoke, out-drink, and out-think any other well-bred girl in the little town. She could ride and take care of a horse, and knew exactly what to look for in a dog. As her father said, Athene was a good girl with no damn nonsense about her. She was his only child, and after his wife died she was mother, daughter, and son to him.

She had only one secret. This was the only thing of which she had ever been ashamed, or afraid. It was a dream. Normally, Athene didn't dream; she went to bed and pulled down a big, thick, black curtain which rolled up at daybreak, when she awoke, bright like a struck match, and went storming and roaring about her daily business—which was the strenuous business of organized pleasure. It would have humiliated her to admit that she had dreams that troubled her.

From time to time—especially after a hard day's hunting—she would drop into a deeper sleep than usual and, although this sleep was terribly deep, she felt until the last that she was somehow standing aside from herself and watching herself. The dream took this form:

She dreamt that she had been asleep. Something at the back of her mind told her that she had been travelling, and was a long way from home. As, in the dream, she came out of a deep blackness, with something like the gasp of relief of a swimmer who comes up to the surface from somewhere below his depth, she knew that she was in a remote and strange place, and that she was in danger.

In her dream she lay still and waited. Athene was an intelligent girl, accustomed to the frenzied patience of the hunter and the fisherman: she knew how to keep still.

She knew that she was dreaming, but she wanted to know what was to come.

Her eyes were open. She could see the foot-rail of a black iron bed. Beyond it stood a blank white-washed wall. She could not move her eyes, yet something informed her that, on the north side of the room, directly opposite the window, there stood a lectern with a small vase containing four dying chrysanthemums.

As she reached this stage of the dream the horror of the grave and the fear of death took hold of her, and she wanted to scream. But she couldn't scream.

She was paralysed. Athene was well aware that outside the sun blazed, and that there she would be free and happy. Here there was no sun. This place was dead. One white-hot bar of

light had poked itself between the bars of the window and made a little puddle somewhere behind her. She couldn't see it but she knew it was there; she couldn't move her eyes.

But she could hear.

She could hear little quiet feet approaching. Their scuffling began as a whisper, turned into a flapping, and at last became footsteps which stopped outside the door.

She heard the door-knob turn.

Slippered feet slapped the clean floor. Then she saw two little old ladies dressed in washed-out pale blue, who walked to the foot of the bed.

At this point she awoke, always wet and cold, biting off the beginning of a scream, because it would have been improper for such a woman to express terror, let alone scream.

Athene married. She bore her husband three children, two girls and a boy. Only one of her children went wrong—the girl, who went to live in sin with a politician who afterwards made a fortune out of advertising and thereby vindicated himself. Athene had never said anything about her hideous dream. The time had passed. She was desperately lonely. Her children were strangers to her and she could find no means of loving her husband. She went away.

She did not know where she was going; she knew simply, that she wanted to go away, anywhere away from her world.

She took the train. It was filled with soldiers. Athene had taken a ticket to the end of the line and was prepared to get out anywhere at all. The train was hot and stuffy; they had been crossing a great white desert—white because it was of fine sand under a white-hot sun.

It seemed to her that she read BERGVILLE on the sign in the station and she got out and drank ice-cold beer until the groan of coaches and the screeching of the wheels told her that the train had left without her, so she sent a telegram ahead, dealing with her luggage, found a hotel and went to sleep.

Athene slept heavily, and, as it always happened in her heavy sleeps, she had her dream.

She dreamt that she was in a strange town. She knew that she had missed her train. Athene had not the slightest doubt concerning what was to come; she had dreamt this dream too often before. She knew that she was going to have her nightmare of the white-washed room and the iron bed.

Surely enough, the dream came . . . There she lay, rigid on the iron bed in the white-washed room, unable to move. Athene knew—having dreamed this dream a hundred times before—that she was going to hear footsteps in the passage.

She heard them. They were the old familiar shuffling footsteps that she had associated with the quiet old women in blue.

Athene was aware that she was dreaming, and that in a second or two she would be properly awake, laughing at herself and preparing to go out with the Chesterfield Hunt. So, in spite of the nightmare, she stayed calm.

She heard the footsteps approaching, heard the door open and heard the door close, strained her fixed eyes until the two old ladies in blue came into her field of vision, and then expected to wake up with a terrified shriek, as usual.

But she didn't wake up.

The dream continued:

The two old ladies in blue did not stop. Looking at each other and sadly shaking their heads, they advanced. One of them, with a dry and tremulous forefinger, closed Athene's eyes, and she heard one of the old women say to the other:

'What a lovely corpse she makes. I wonder where she comes from.'

And Athene knew that, when she awoke this time, no one would ever hear her scream.

Scottish Melody

SHEILA LAVELLE

I used to keep on having this horrible dream. It varies a bit but it usually goes like this. You've been given the star part in a famous play and you're up on stage on the opening night. Your leading man is that drop-dead-gorgeous young lad off *Coronation Street* and he's already invited you to have supper with him after the show. The theatre is stuffed with people, buzzing with excitement, and loads of well-known celebrities are in the audience. Sometimes even the Queen.

The lights dim. The curtain rises. A hush descends. You're in the middle of the stage and everybody is watching you, waiting for you to speak. You open your mouth but nothing comes out because *you've forgotten your lines*. The silence grows longer and longer and your face turns as red as a smacked backside as you stand there with your mouth opening and shutting like a penguin that's dropped its fish.

It makes you go hot and cold all over, doesn't it? I used to wake up sweating and groaning with my heart banging about under the pussycat pyjamas my gran sent me from Glasgow for Christmas.

It's funny though. I don't get that dream any more. I haven't had it for ages. Not since the ghastly thing that happened to me at the Sunny Sands Holiday Park in Ayrshire this summer. That was a nightmare to beat them all.

It wasn't my idea to invite my cousin Caroline to come with us on holiday. All I wanted to do was go for long walks by the sea with my black-and-white collie Puccini, or just curl up with a book, or practise my violin if the weather was bad. Caroline would want to drag me around shops and cinemas and funfairs and discos and flirt with horrible pimply boys. She would spoil everything.

'Don't be daft, Annie,' said my dad, as he filled in the booking form for a three-bedroomed holiday chalet at Sunny Sands. 'Caroline will be great company for you. She'll get you out and about meeting people, instead of all this mooning about in your room. It'll do you the world of good.'

He sealed the envelope and stuck on the stamp. 'Come on, bonnie lass,' he said, smiling at the grim expression on my face. 'You know Mum and I will have to spend all our time with Gran. You don't want to trail around with three old fogies like us, do you?'

Trailing around with a man-eating tiger would be better than having Caroline for company, I thought bitterly. Last time we went on holiday together she put hairy dead spiders in everybody's beds and said it was me. But in the end I had to give in. Have you noticed how parents get their own way by saying it'll do you the world of good? And when I argued Mum just put her foot down and told me to stop moaning or they'd leave me behind. So that was that.

At first it wasn't too bad. It didn't take long to drive from Newcastle to Glasgow to pick up Gran and Caroline. Uncle Joe and Aunt Marion gave us a huge lunch, and loads of hugs and kisses when we left, delighted no doubt to be getting rid of not only Gran for a week but Caroline as well.

Caroline was dead friendly and chatty on the way down the coast to Ayr, even if she did take up most of the space in the back seat, and I began to relax a bit. The chalet at Sunny Sands was roomy and bright, and Caroline and Poochy and I shared a twin-bedded room at the back, looking out over woods and fields and a brilliant cliff-top path. We made the most of that, Poochy and I.

'Oh, lord. You and that mangy dog,' Caroline would complain, whenever she saw him bouncing up and down like a yo-yo while I tried to put on his lead. 'Don't you ever get sick of all this trudging about in the rain?'

I never got sick of it at all. And I was glad the weather had turned out so dismal because it meant that nobody else wanted to come with me. They went away every day on coachtrips to stately homes, or to eat in posh restaurants and hotels, and they spent every evening in the clubhouse where there was a stage with singers and comedians and a live rock bank. Poochy and I were left to go walking and to share our take-away fish and chips or fried chicken or beefburgers in peace, and I got to practise my violin and read paperback novels and listen to my music tapes as much as I pleased.

Caroline made friends with a gang of kids from Paisley, and she soon stopped trying to drag me along to discos and things. My skinny figure and my specs and my baggy old jumpers and jeans may have had something to do with that, but I didn't care. I had better things to do than cover my face with clarty make-up and chase after a load of boys.

It was on the Thursday morning when we were all having breakfast together in the chalet that Gran came up with her awful idea.

'Annie, pet, you should enter the Young Talent Contest tomorrow night in the clubhouse,' she said. She nodded towards my violin on the sideboard where my dad had left it after tuning it for me. 'You're getting real good on that fiddle.' She poked a bit of bacon from her toothless gums and looked round at the others knowingly. 'Good as Nigel Kennedy, she is. I've heard her practising.'

'No way!' I said, horrified. 'I'm not nearly good enough to play in public. And anyway, they'll want pop songs and stuff like that. Who'll want to listen to Mozart or Vivaldi in a place like this?'

And I buttered myself another slice of toast, knowing I must sound like a terrible snob, but hoping that would be the end of the matter.

'What about that Scottish melody you play?' said Caroline, getting up to re-fill the teapot. 'You know. The one with five or six different tunes all strung together. I bet that would go down a bomb around here.' She hummed a few bars of 'The Bluebells of Scotland' and started dancing about on the lino by the sink.

I looked down my nose at her. 'You mean medley, not melody, stupid,' I said scornfully, but she only laughed.

'Well, whatever,' she said, tossing her long hair out of her eyes like a pony shaking off flies. 'I still think it's a great idea.'

I could see that my mum and dad thought so too.

'It would be a wonderful opportunity for you to play for a proper audience,' my mum said. 'So far you've only played for the school.'

My dad reached out and ruffled my hair. 'Go on, sweetheart,' he said. 'Give it a go. It'll do you the world of good.'

In my heart I knew he was right. I had to start somewhere, and playing in public here, where nobody knew me, would be far less nerve-racking than playing for an audience of neighbours and friends back home in Newcastle.

'OK. I'll do it,' I said, and they all cheered as if I'd won a gold medal in the Olympics.

'Good lass,' said my dad, and went rushing off to get an entry form. Caroline set up my music stand and fetched my sheets of music, while Mum and Gran cleared away the breakfast things, creeping about respectfully so I wouldn't be disturbed.

I had only been practising for five minutes when I had a sudden thought. 'Oh, heck. What'll I wear?' I wailed, scowling down at my old jeans and trainers which were the only kind of things I'd brought with me. 'Everybody'll be dressed up all posh. I can't go like this.'

They gazed at one another in dismay. Caroline looked me up and down, and a strange expression came into her eyes.

'You can borrow my new black satin skirt,' she said suddenly. 'And my red top with the sequins on it. You'll look fab with your lovely dark hair.'

I stared at her in surprise. She had been saving that skirt and that sequinned top for the party on the last night, and for her to offer them to me was unbelievable. Maybe I'd been wrong about her all along. It was the most unselfish thing I had ever known her do.

'Well,' I said uncertainly. 'The top would be OK, because I like things loose rather than tight. But the skirt might be a bit too big around the waist.' I didn't like to point out that she was vastly overweight and looked like Humpty Dumpty before he went on a diet. A skirt that fitted her would go round me twice. But she already had the answer.

'Don't worry, Annie,' she said smiling. 'I've thought about that. I can easily turn the waistband over and thread some elastic through.' She grinned at Gran cheekily. 'I bet Gran has some spare knicker elastic with her,' she said. 'You never go anywhere without it, do you, Gran?'

Gran cackled and chomped her gums as if she were chewing the cud. 'Ee, hinny, you're dead right there,' she said. 'You never know when it might come in handy.'

Caroline fetched the skirt and began to sew a slot in the waistband. I got back to my practising, much to the disgust of Poochy, who had been hoping for a walk. He crawled under the sideboard and put his paws over his nose. I bet he would have put his paws over his ears if he could.

All that day and the next I practised like mad, with breaks only for meals and walking the dog, and by seven o'clock on the Friday evening my Scottish Medley sounded really good, even if I do say it myself. I played the first three tunes in a lilting, jaunty style which suited the music, then switched to a sadder, more plaintive effect for numbers four and five. My dad clapped enthusiastically after listening to my last rehearsal.

'That's bloomin' marvellous, Annie,' he said, and I'm sure there were tears in his eyes. He used to play violin in a jazz band in Gateshead until he injured his left hand in an accident at work. His middle finger doesn't bend properly any more, but he's still got a better ear than me for pitch. I've always let either him or my teacher tune the violin for me ever since I started to learn.

He took it from me to do so now. 'You'll knock 'em for six,' he beamed. 'Let's just give that fiddle a final tune-up before we go.' And he started twanging and twiddling the pegs to adjust the strings.

'I'm not letting her put this skirt on till the very last minute, mind,' warned Caroline bossily. 'It's satin and it shows every mark. She can go in trousers and change before she goes on stage.' She started folding the skirt and putting it in a carrier bag.

That seemed to make sense, so I put on my baggy jeans and Caroline's sparkly red top and brushed my hair out loose over my shoulders. I settled Poochy in his basket with a couple of Bonios and gave him a hug. My dad picked up my violin case and we all walked together up the road to the clubhouse.

My stomach jumped and bounced as if it were full of goldfish when I saw the crowds of people thronging the entrance. Given half a chance I'd have turned tail and scooted off back to Poochy. But my dad was taking charge.

'Contestant,' he announced importantly, ushering me past the queue and in through the door, and everyone fell back and stared at us as we went in. A tall thin woman with grey wiry hair like rows of Brillo pads was ticking off names on a paper clipped to a board.

'Annie Wilson,' I told her, my voice coming out in a squeak. She didn't seem to hear me, so Caroline took over.

'This is Annie Wilson, the violinist,' she declared loudly. 'And I'm her dresser and personal assistant.' She waved the bag with the skirt in it to prove it, and Brillo-head ticked my name on her list.

'You're last. Number ten,' she informed me, and she pointed towards a row of seats near the stage where the other competitors were already beginning to gather.

'Parents at the back of the hall, please,' she added curtly, and I clung to my dad for a moment in panic.

'There, there, bonny lass,' he soothed. 'Don't fret. You're gonna be just grand.' He opened the case, held the violin close to his ear and plucked the strings to check again that they were still in tune. 'Spot on,' he said, handing the case back to me. 'Go for it, our Annie.'

I watched as my mum and dad and gran made their way to a table near the back.

Caroline grabbed my arm and yanked me off to the row of performers. We sat down next to a fat pale boy in evening dress and a bow tie, who was peering at a sheet of music and humming '*O Sole Mio*' under his breath.

'Shall I go and change into the skirt?' I hissed at Caroline, but she shook her head.

'Good lord, no,' she said. 'You're not on till last. You've got a couple of hours before you need to do that.' I wasn't too happy sitting there in my jeans, I can tell you, but apart from wrestling with her for the bag there wasn't a lot I could do.

The hall rapidly filled with talking, laughing, shouting people, greeting friends and buying each other drinks. The seats weren't set out in rows, but arranged in groups round little tables, and there was a bar at the back of the hall where I could see my dad being served with a pint of beer. Caroline kept waving at her pals from Paisley who were giggling and nudging each other right at the front, and I couldn't help wondering why she should choose to be with me rather than them.

Suddenly there was a hush as an incredibly tall thin man in tight leather trousers and an orange vest to match his hair walked up the steps onto the stage.

'Welcome to tonight's Young Talent Contest,' he bawled into the microphone, making it screech and buzz. 'We've got plenty of talented youngsters for you this evening, ladies and gentlemen, so let's give them all a round of applause.' He flashed his big white teeth as the audience began to clap and cheer.

I had to sit through nearly two hours of torture, my stomach churning like a bucket of worms, as the other contestants went through their acts. Three of them were girl singers, doing pop songs from the top ten to their own taped accompaniments, and the audience loved them all. There were two stand-up comedians who both told the same boring old jokes that could only have come out of the *Beano*. There was a boy ventriloquist whose puppet was an enormous hedgehog called Cuddles. There was the operatic tenor who sang '*O Sole Mio*' as if he were being strangled. There was a clown who juggled and rode a one-wheeled bike and fell about all over the stage. There was a girl in a kilt who did real Scottish dancing to a tape of bagpipes and drums. And then there was me.

Caroline at last rushed me off to the girls' dressing room shortly before the end of the act before mine. I wriggled out of my jeans and she pulled the black satin skirt over my head.

'It's still too big!' I shrieked as it slid straight down to my feet. Caroline giggled.

'I haven't fastened the elastic yet, you clot,' she said. 'I left the ends loose till you got it on. Stand still will you, while I tie the knot.'

She pulled the skirt back up round my waist and yanked at the two ends of elastic which were hanging out of the waistband at the back. I felt the satin bunch up as it gathered round me. 'There. Howzat feel?' said Caroline, and I nodded. I could hear the applause as the Scottish dancer ended, and I knew there was no time to spare.

'It's fine,' I gasped hurriedly. 'Come on, we have to go.'

Caroline used to be a Girl Guide so she's good at knots. She quickly finished tying the elastic and pushed me through the door. 'Right,' she said. 'You get on stage fast while I fetch your violin and bow.'

Mr Orange Vest was just beginning to announce me when I reached the wings.

'Ladeez and gentlemen,' he bellowed, holding up his hand for silence. 'A warm welcome please for our last performer of the evening. The violinist, Miss Anneeee Wilson!'

The audience broke into applause once more as I walked out into the middle of the stage. As I walked I thought I felt the elastic round my waist slip just a bit, but there was no time to worry about that now. I was frantically watching Caroline as she dragged the instrument case out from under the seat where we'd left it. She took out the violin and bent over it for a moment, her back to me. What the heck could be taking her so long? Come on, Caroline, I prayed silently. I knew I must look a right twit standing there, a violinist without a violin.

Old Orange Vest thought so too, I could tell. He stared at me and consulted his list with a puzzled frown.

'Er, Annie is going to play for us a Scottish, er, Melody,' he announced, then he suddenly beamed in relief as Caroline bounded up the steps and shoved the violin and bow into my hands.

'Medley, not melody,' I said with a sigh. But the audience now waited quietly for me to begin, so with a quick bow he followed Caroline off the stage.

I launched into 'The Bluebells of Scotland' and I had only played a few bars when I realized that something was wrong. I stopped, gave a nervous grin at the audience, and started again.

Maybe it was something to do with the acoustics in the hall, or the temperature or something, and it would settle down if I carried on. But a few more bars of the most horrible cacophony you ever heard convinced me. My violin was *out of tune*.

I don't know whether you've ever heard an out-of-tune violin, but it would make a caterwauling cat sound like Pavarotti. 'The Bluebells of Scotland' was only just recognizable, and halfway through it I heard somebody start to boo. I looked down and there was Caroline, sitting with her Paisley pals, cupping her mouth with both hands and shouting 'Boo! Get 'er off!' while her friends fell about laughing and clutched one another in ecstasy. I only needed one look at Caroline's sly grin and I knew what she had done.

I ploughed desperately on, calling myself all the rude names I could think of for not learning to tune the violin myself, and praying that my dad would come to my rescue. I saw him struggling to get up from his seat, but people round him were laughing and pulling him down. Even my mum and gran were smiling, and that's when I saw that nobody else had joined in with Caroline's boos. To my complete and utter astonishment, everybody seemed to think my rendering of 'The Bluebells of Scotland' was the funniest thing they'd ever heard. They rocked with laughter in their seats, clapped their hands in time with the music, and some boys in the front even whistled and stamped their feet.

In a sort of daze I changed key and began to play the most discordant version of 'Loch Lomond' you ever heard. My face was scarlet and I was shaking all over with rage and humiliation, but the audience seemed to be loving every minute so there was nothing I could do but carry on. But as I played I was becoming more and more alarmed by the elastic round my waist, which seemed to be getting looser the more I stretched and bent my bow arm. And I couldn't hitch my skirt up because I needed both hands to play.

The audience howled with delight when I finished 'Loch Lomond' and started the dancing rhythm of 'Donald Where's Yer Troozers'. They clapped, stamped their feet, and joined in with the words at the tops of their voices, while I played numbly on, trying not to move my arms too much as the skirt grew looser and looser around my waist.

'Annie Laurie' was a dreary wailing dirge, but it almost brought the house down, and when I struck into 'Auld Lang Syne' everybody crossed their arms and joined hands and sang their hearts out. I gazed over the heads of the crowd to see my dad roaring his head off just like everybody else. Even he thought I was doing it on purpose, so I kept on playing gamely to the end even though the dreadful noise I was making was hurting my ears.

The last notes of 'Auld Lang Syne' died away and my Scottish Medley was over at last. To tumultuous applause I made my final bow. And that's when the knot in the elastic slipped altogether and Caroline's skirt went slithering down over my hips towards my knees. I shrieked, flung away my bow, and snatched up the skirt with my free hand, just in time to prevent everyone from getting an eyeful of my Marks and Spencer's underwear. Somehow I managed to stumble off the stage into the wings, while the audience went wild, clapping and cheering, whistling and stamping, and shouting 'Bravo!'

I put the violin on the floor while I pulled my skirt back up. I slid the knot in the elastic round from the back to the front to have a look. And then I said a very rude word. My dear ex-Girl-Guide cousin had tied the ends together in a slip knot, knowing that my movements as I played would be enough for it gradually to work itself loose. I was wondering how I would ever get my revenge when I realized that the audience had embarked on a rhythmic clapping and were shouting 'Ann-ee! Ann-ee!' in the hope that I would reappear. So I quickly pulled the elastic tight, tied it very firmly in a double reef knot and walked back on stage to pick up my bow.

The talent contest was judged by the amount of applause each act had received, so there was no doubt in anybody's mind that the winner was me. Old Orange Vest was still laughing when he presented me with an envelope stuffed with a hundred pounds in tenners and fivers.

'A great act, ladies and gentlemen,' he bellowed. 'The funniest thing I've seen for a long time. Another big hand please for Anneeee Wilson!'

I glanced down at Caroline, and seeing the sick expression on her face was all the revenge I would ever need. I ignored her completely when I left the stage to thread my way through the crowd to my family's table. I got my dad to order a bottle of champagne and four glasses, and Caroline didn't even get a sip. So what had started as a nightmare had a happy ending, after all.

I still dream about it though, and wake up sweating and groaning with my heart banging about under my pussycat pyjamas. But at least it's taught me a lesson. I've now learnt how to tune a violin.

Mrs Beale and Trixie

CHRISTOPHER LEACH

He had burned badly. His face had a tattered look: a mixture of gold stubble and strips of tissue-like skin which, having once drawn blood, he now left alone. The pack, heavier each day, dug its straps into his shoulders, and that old dream of being a free and roaming man—at one with Brother Sun and Sister Moon—brought only a short angry laugh, a snort, at that youth who had started out with a face as smooth as a child's, to walk the world; or, at least today, the Dorset coastline.

Now he turned his back on the molten sea and sought somewhere to sleep for the night: the thought of a cool, curtained room, cool sheets, and a cold pillow in which to sink his throbbing face, urging his weary body forward.

The fields, wilting with summer, burned an acid yellow-green. The air seemed made of fine-meshed straw: he could taste its dryness, smell its furnace breath. He gasped. Swallowed, with no relief. He bent his head under the weight of the sun, and the sharp gravel of the road glared and winked its thousand sparks. He closed his eyes, his boots slipping on the sudden gradient leading down to the village.

Once he was on the flat again, he opened his eyes. Houses were suffocating under heavy, motionless trees. Hot shadows and flies. Tormented horses shuddered near fences; and a foal lay twitching in deep grass. He went to the plank bungalow and rang the bell.

Two people came: the man behind the woman. Old and curious: an event in their Sunday, a disturbance in those hot rooms. 'You are in a state,' said the woman. 'Look at his face, Gordon.'

'Caught the sun,' said the man.

'I'm looking for bed and breakfast,' he said. 'Just for one night.'

'Sorry,' said the woman. 'We don't do any. We did once upon a time. But people take advantage. Mrs Crawford does, sometimes. Want a drink of water? Go and get him a drink, Gordon.'

The old man went slowly away.

'Where does she live: Mrs Crawford?'

'Being fair, you'd catch it more,' said the woman. 'You ought to 've known that. She lives in the one with the thatch, opposite the church. To the left.'

Heavy, gold-dusted bees sang between them: a sound full of sleep. He opened his eyes again to the glass, the beads of water on the old man's hand. He drank; and it was beautiful.

'Thank you,' he said.

'Come far?' said the old man.

'London.'

'I went there . . . once,' he said. 'Didn't think much of it. Try Mrs Beale.'

'Don't start that,' said the woman.

The old man giggled.

'Make her day, it would. He's about the same age.'

'I said leave it,' said the woman. She nodded at the distance. 'You try Mrs Crawford. Sleep in a field, I would. The weather for it.'

'I've had enough of fields,' he said. 'Thank you.'

As he turned away he heard the woman say:

'Why'd you say that—about Mrs Beale? You love making trouble, don't you?'

Mrs Crawford, younger, prettier; children at her skirt in the flower-starred garden, pointed to the two bicycles resting against the wall. 'Them's staying,' she said. 'Sorry.' She looked away from his face. 'Try Minster. Get yourself a lift.'

'How far's that?'

'Six miles,' she said. 'Plenty there.'

'What about Mrs Beale?'

Her face sharpened. 'What about Mrs Beale? Don't make it worse. Who told you? The Vails?'

'Two old people. In the bungalow.'

'You leave her alone,' said Mrs Crawford. 'You . . . you sleep in the open. Don't worry Mrs Beale.'

She pushed the children towards the house.

Two boys were sailing paper boats in the weed-mapped duck-pond. Large hats shadowed their faces. Flies glowed on the brims. Their eyes were quick and sharp as lizards.

'What you want her for?' said one.

'Don't tell him,' said the other. 'He don't come from around here.'

'Sign says *Ice Cream*,' said the first. 'She lives there. She don't sell ice cream, though. Used to.'

'Where's that?'

The second boy slapped at the green water with a long stick.

'Leave her alone,' he said.

The other boy pointed, grinning.

'Over there. In all those trees.'

The second boy slapped the water harder.

'Well?' said the first. 'No harm, is there?'

It was an old sign. Rusty and bleached by the seasons. Almost hidden by ivy and fiery tendrils. *Walls Ice Cream* in pale, raised letters. A whisper of words. It hung by one nail, lopsided, at the start of an overgrown driveway; and he could see the roof of a house, a tall chimney. He walked past a gate latched with weeds, dry moss under his boots, flies feeding on his sweat.

There was a sudden fluttering, as though doves clustered about the door of the house. And then he saw that they were pieces of paper: a mass of them, pinned to the framework, stirred by a funnel of air, which died. He crossed the small, thick lawn and looked at them. They were letters, notes, messages: addressed to kings and emperors and Jesus and God and the local council. Some were old: the ink fading, the pins discoloured. Others more recent: pleas for justice and fair play. And all concerning the return of a son.

He crouched lower, reading them. To a dry, crisp, *tick-tick*, like the sound of a small, busy clock the door of the house was nosed open and a dog appeared. A white greyhound. But a greyhound no longer lean: a barrel of a body on thin, incongruous legs. It came forward and sniffed at his boots. Then it went back, pushed the door wider, and the tick-tick of its paws faded on the tiles of the hall.

He took another quick glance at the papers. *My life's-blood spilled. Left to rot in my old age, alone. Who answers me? none.*

He turned away. He would find a field, a barn: take a chance again with the mice, the unexplained rustles in the dark.

'Greg?' a voice asked.

She was a big woman, country-woman's arms bare and freckled, her body tight in a faded pinafore, and tied. Tight grey curls like wire, rouge on each cheek, thin wire spectacles over weak bird-eyes, peering. 'That you, Greg?'

'No.'

Her teeth browning as she smiled. Feet in scuffed red mules, inching forward.

'Where've you been all this time?'

'I'm sorry, I have . . . I have the wrong house.'

The dog came and looked up at him and whined softly, the thin rat-like tail beating.

'Who is it, Trixie?' she said. 'Is it our Greg?'

'I was looking for Mrs Crawford.'

'What for?'

'It . . . doesn't matter.'

'You don't want her. You stay here with me.' Her strong hand touched, held his arm. 'You're still as thin as ever. Didn't they feed you right?' Her face came closer: a map of lines, creasing.

'What've you done to your face? They do that to you?'

'I've caught the sun, that's all.'

'You always did. Always had sensitive skin. Carried you off the beach that day, remember? Need some cream on that, you do. Come in. And welcome home.'

The coolness of the hall, the house, tempted him. Faint with the heat, he longed for rest. To close his eyes, and drift. If only for a few minutes. To rest.

The dog followed after. Tick-tick-tick.

Old prints. Country scenes in dark frames. A blacksmith at his forge. Children gathering bluebells. A faint smell of . . . polish?

'Come into the kitchen,' she said. He noticed now that she limped, swinging a stiff left leg out from her body, and back. Her hand on the wall, trailing. 'You're not just on leave, are you? You don't have to go back?'

'I'm not . . . Greg.'

'Good,' she said. 'I'm glad you're out of it, at last. I've waited long enough.'

She swung herself past the table, and opened a small cabinet fixed to the wall. She took out a tube of cream. He held out his hand.

'Thank you,' he said.

'Sit down. I'll do it. You can't see where it's needed.'

'I can look in that mirror.'

'Don't fuss, Greg. Sit down.'

He sat down. She took the cap off the cream, and pressed some on to her fingertips. As soon as he felt her touch on his face he experienced a beautiful sense of calm, of peace. His weary shoulders relaxed. He closed his eyes.

'Tsk tsk,' she said softly. 'What a state to get in, eh, Trixie?'

Her fingers moved lightly over his burned skin. He knew he would remember the cheap over-sweet smell of the cream for the rest of his life.

'There,' she said, again as softly as a whisper: 'how's that?'

'Great,' he said opening his eyes. Her face was very close, full of tenderness. 'Thanks.'

'It oughtn't to be allowed,' she said, straightening. 'They ought to take more care of you boys. It was the same in the first war, with your dad. Treat men like sheep; cattle. Still, you're home now. All forgiven and forgotten. What do you want to do first? Tea? Nice cup of tea?'

'I wouldn't mind a nap.'

'Hot day sends us all to sleep,' she said. 'And you've come a long way.' She touched his sleeve. 'I never believed that telegram, those letters. I knew you wasn't dead. Knew you'd come back. Kept your old room like always. Just waiting.'

It was very clean. Very tidy. Waiting for him. Yet there was a staleness in the air, a hot stuffiness. A wasp knocked and knocked against the glass of one of the windows. Straight lines everywhere; a loving precision. Smoothed.

'Hasn't been touched,' she said. ''Cept for the cleaning. Every day, first thing. Pleased?'

'Yes.'

She opened the window and the wasp sang free. The stifled calls of summer sounded: cows and drowsy cuckoos. She pulled back the covers of the bed. 'Nice to have you home again, son.'

He gave her a slight smile: too tired to argue. A short sleep, and he'd be fit for the road again.

'Got a kiss for your mother?' she said.

He moved as in a warm fog, and kissed her cheek. She patted his arm. 'You have a nice sleep, Greg. I'll get a lovely tea ready for you. All your favourites. Come along, Trixie.' The dog whined, placing its front paws on the bed. 'Wants to stay with you, like always. Want her?'

He looked down at the dog. The large, bulging, over-bright eyes unnerved him.

'No,' he said.

'You come now, Trixie,' she said. 'Plenty of time to make friends again. All the time in the world.' She ushered the dog out, and began to close the door. 'I'll wake you about six.'

'Yes.'

The door closed. He stood there, shivering with tiredness, the weight of the invisible pack cutting into his shoulders. And fell on to the bed.

He lifted his head. Beyond him was the shattered farmhouse, sunlight catching a sudden wink of metal.

'How many, do you think?' said a voice.

He brought down his head and looked to his right. The old-young officer's face, very near, was rinsed with sweat.

'I don't know, sir,' he said. 'Can't tell until we . . .'

'Yes, of course,' said the officer. 'Right, you men—forward, slowly. Take advantage of any cover. No firing, until told.'

The ground was hard, aching for rain. Flies fed on their faces, throats, hands. The farmhouse shifted nearer. Again that sudden wink of metal. Didn't they realize . . . ?

Nearer still. There were hens, undisturbed, going about their business. Peaceful. Bluster of bees.

'Stay,' said the officer. 'Right, Jenkins and Beale: round the back, to the left.' Resting his right arm on the earth, he wiped the sweat from his eyes and looked at his watch. 'We go in at . . . ten to. Agreed? OK, move . . .'

The walls of the farmhouse were continents of faded whitewash: oceans and coastlines, merging. Dry white grass. A hen clucked, moved away.

The second hand ticked on. Sun reflected in the glass; gone.

'Dying of thirst, I am 'ere,' said Jenkins. 'Hope they . . .'

'Welcome,' said a voice.

His stomach seemed to drain away, leaving only the lurch of his heart. The face behind the flame-thrower was smiling.

He fumbled at his Sten.

He heard Jenkins cry:

'Don't! Don't, please! Oh, Jesus, don't . . .'

The black barrels spouted. Fierce, acrid, roaring, screaming gouts of flame ripped the air, and punched into his body. His life, his childhood, fears, desires, were being eaten alive. He smelled his burning uniform; and then his own flesh, cooking. His hair was full of little crackling voices. He heard Jenkins screaming . . . or was it himself?

Diving rolling shouting: still the flames ate into him.

'GodJesusMother!' he heard someone call. 'Mother! Mum!'

He opened his eyes. There was a dusty pattern of leaves and roses. It was a carpet. Dusty smell of . . . what? Her hands were trying to lift him. He turned on his back and looked up at her. The dog danced around.

'Nightmare,' she said. 'A terrible nightmare.' There were tears in her eyes. 'What did they do to you, Greg? You poor boy.'

He struggled to rise.

'Must've fallen . . . off the bed,' he said. 'Sorry.'

'You were screaming,' she said. She pushed his hair off his wet forehead. 'Poor thing.'

He sighed. 'I'm all right now.'

'A bath would freshen you up,' she said. 'Want a bath?'

To soak. To let all the heat slip from his body. To be clean.

'Yes, I'd like one,' he said.

'Dressing-gown in the usual place,' she said. 'You get those clothes off. I'll get it ready. Come on, Trixie. Out we go.'

He opened the cupboard and took out the towelled dressing-gown. It smelled of mothballs: a homely smell. He sank his face into it. And then he undressed.

He felt better after he had bathed: his body lighter, more in his control. Using the towel, he saw himself in the mirror: his body so white, his face and hands those of another man—a dark sun-struck man, strong in contrast to the white weakling who looked away from the ravaged features, the flayed skin.

His clothes were gone from the bed, replaced by clean, folded pyjamas. He went out on to the landing.

'My clothes?' he shouted.

The dog came skittering up the stairs, to dance around him.

She came out of the kitchen. 'What, love?'

'My clothes?'

'They need washing,' she said. 'You can wear your grey suit tomorrow. Wear the pyjamas for now. Cooler. Tea's waiting for you.'

The dog followed him into the bedroom.

'Oh, get lost!' he said.

But it leapt on to the bed, and lay happily, tongue lolling.

He put on the pyjamas, tightened the cord. The creases were sharp, as though they had waited years. He shrugged back into the dressing-gown, smoothed his hair; and went downstairs, the dog scrambling after him.

She was waiting for him in the kitchen, standing behind the laden table. She had changed into a blue gingham dress, and had threaded a blue ribbon through the wire of her curls.

'That's better,' she said. 'You look rested.'

'I am, yes. A nice tea.'

'I bet you're hungry. You always had a good appetite. Everything you like: ham, cucumber, celery, beetroot—with plenty of vinegar. The tomatoes and the lettuce are ours. We . . .'

There was a soft tap at the front door, and the dog ran to investigate.

A voice said: 'May I come in, Mrs Beale?'

She moved around the table and looked down the hall.

'Yes, come in, vicar,' she said. 'Come in the kitchen. Time for a cup of tea.'

'Not that I time myself,' the voice said. 'I rarely . . .'

The vicar entered: a tall, stooping man with a rock-like face topped by stiff grey hair. The white clerical collar sharp below the weathered, furrowed cheeks. The face thrust forward now, the eyes moving over the dressing-gown, the pyjamas, the bare feet.

'I see you have company,' he said, slowly. 'I won't . . .'

'Don't say company,' said Mrs Beale, smiling. 'You could say a celebration. I'd like you to meet my son—Greg. Back home at last.'

'Your son?' said the vicar. 'But, Mrs Beale . . .'

'All that talking we did—or you did: didn't matter, did it? Faith and hope: that's all it needed. Like I said.'

The vicar's face was growing more rock-like.

'Your son, you say?' he said. 'You're . . . certain?'

'Wouldn't I know my own son?' said Mrs Beale, a tremor in her voice. 'In a prisoner-of-war camp; or a hospital, wasn't you, Greg? Look at his face, vicar—what he's been through.'

'Perhaps I could have a word with him alone for a moment, Mrs Beale,' said the vicar. 'I'd like to . . .'

'I don't trust you,' she said. 'I'll stay here. You say what you like to him.'

'Who are you?' said the vicar. 'I don't want any pretence about this. Mrs Beale has . . .'

'He's my son!' she said, swiftly. 'I'd know him, wouldn't I?' The tremor was back in her voice, and she held tightly to the back of a chair. 'Don't you come in here, telling me it's impossible. I told you—I always told you—he'd be back. If you're going to start that again . . .'

'I'm starting nothing, Mrs Beale,' said the vicar. He seemed to come to a decision. 'I'll . . . I'll leave you to your tea. I'm so glad he's back. I'll see you both later.'

'No, you won't go like that,' she said. 'I don't need to be protected any more. I don't need your friends looking in. You still don't believe me, do you?' She turned. 'Tell him who you are.'

He looked from her triumphant face to the vicar's hardness. He opened his mouth.

'Tell him, Greg,' she said.

'I'm her son,' he said.

'Tell him where you've been.'

'In . . . in hospital.'

'See?' she said.

'Yes, I see,' said the vicar. 'Well . . . I *will* see you both later.'

He went out, a black tower of a man, into the hall, and the evening sunlight.

The knife rested on the loaf. 'More?' she said.

'No, thank you.'

'Had enough?'

'More than enough,' he said. 'It was a great tea.'

She put down the knife and leaned back in her chair.

'What you going to do with yourself now?' she said. 'You're not going back to Arnold's, are you?'

He felt a sudden terror at the blank spaces. 'I . . .'

'I don't want you back there,' she said. 'No place for you— never was. You're not a farming boy. You've got more in you than that.' She pushed herself out of the chair and went to a small cupboard, grunted down, opened the door, and brought something out. 'Recognize it?'

It was a large tin, decorated with castles and knights.

'I . . .'

She sat back, smiling, and folded her arms.

'Open it,' she said.

He tugged at the lid, and at last it jerked back. The tin was full of money, crammed with banknotes.

'All yours,' she said. 'Everything I could manage to put by, over the years. To give you a better start. Remember you was mad about engines, cars? What about that lot for a start?'

His fingers moved over the crisp ridges.

'Count it,' she said.

'Now?'

'Go on,' she said. 'Let's see how much we got.'

He took out the notes; and began counting.

He finished in the silence.

'Nearly six hundred,' he said. 'Five hundred and . . . eighty-seven.' He looked up. 'Five hun—'

She was staring directly down the hall, unblinking.

'Mrs Beale?' he said. And then, in a panic: 'Mum?'

She did not move.

He raced around the table, scattering banknotes to the floor. He took her shoulders and shook her. Her head swayed to the left. The eyes still staring. She was dead.

It was then that he heard a commotion in the garden; and then in the hall. The villagers were coming, led by the dark, swift-pacing figure of the vicar. Soon they filled the small kitchen, with others pressing behind. They looked from the dead, staring woman to the notes on the table and on the floor. The open mouth of the tin. And then they turned their heads and looked at him.

And their eyes were burning.

Nightmare

MORGAN LLYWELYN

Something was breathing in the dark.

Peter lay still for a long time, listening. The sound was coming from the far corner of his bedroom, opposite the windows. In that corner was nothing but a straight-backed chair on which he threw his clothes when he undressed. There was no dog in the room, nor even in the house. No creature at all that could be breathing in his bedroom in the middle of the night.

Yet something woke him up. Something that shouldn't be there.

The inhalations were ragged and gasping, the way Peter sounded after he jogged several miles. But the longer he listened, the less human the breathing seemed.

He should turn on the light and see what it was. He was too old to be lying with the bedclothes drawn up to his chin because of some strange noise. If he got out of bed and investigated, he would find it was only one of the normal creaks and groans of an old house at night.

But he didn't turn on the light. He didn't get up, either. Part of him was excited and turning on the light would just spoil the fun.

And part of him—he didn't want to admit this to himself, but it was true—part of him was afraid.

He lay rigid in the bed, listening; starting to sweat.

Maybe this is just a nightmare, he thought. But he didn't believe it.

The breathing continued.

'Who are you?' he finally demanded. Unfortunately his words didn't come out as brave and full of challenge as he intended. His voice quavered, reminding him that it had changed not so very long ago. Embarrassed, he cleared his throat and tried again. 'Who are you? What do you think you're doing in my room?'

No answer, only breathing.

Pitching his voice as deep as it would go, Peter announced sternly, 'I'm going to count to five and then I'm coming over there. You'd better speak up before you make me really mad.'

The breathing became harsher but there was no other response.

Now he had to get up; he couldn't make an empty threat like some little kid. He was in charge here, after all. He had fought for the right to be able to stay by himself, and laughed at Mum when she was uncertain about it. 'I'm practically grown,' he had reminded her. 'I can certainly mind the house for a fortnight.'

The last thing Mum had said before she and Terry left was, 'You will be all right until we get back, Peter—won't you?'

'He will,' Terry had assured her. Then, turning to Peter he had added with a grin, 'I won't let her worry about a thing, I know you'll handle any problems that come up just fine. I have a feeling we're going to be great pals, you and me.'

Mum had been lonely for a long time, but lately she had started to sing in the mornings as she cooked breakfast, and there was a sparkle in her eyes. When she and Terry had left that morning to go on their honeymoon, she looked positively radiant. Until that moment, Peter had never realized his mother was a beautiful woman.

He couldn't disappoint her now. He had to deal with whatever this was, so he threw back the covers and reached for the switch of the bedside lamp. But, like the house, the lamp was old and not in good repair. No matter how he thumbed the switch it wouldn't come on.

Muttering to himself, he slid out of bed. Beneath his blue-striped cotton pyjamas his stomach felt hollow. When his feet touched the floor it creaked so loudly he snatched his feet up again and sat perched on the edge of his bed like some great bird. Then he was angry with himself. He felt like a fool.

It was all the fault of the house, of course.

He had disliked the place from the beginning. It was a tired old farmhouse with a roof that sagged in the middle and some sort of dying vine clinging to the gable end like a drowning man clinging to a rock. The paint was peeling and the rooms smelled damp. But when Mum and Terry had brought him out here to see it for the first time, their faces had glowed as if they'd done something wonderful.

Peter, however, had been dismayed. 'You're buying a house next to an old *cemetery*? That's crazy!'

'No it isn't, it makes good sense, son,' Terry had replied calmly. Peter hated it when Terry called him 'son', but the older man never seemed to notice. 'Because of the location we're having to pay less than we would for the same house anywhere else. It may seem sort of shabby right now, but you and I together can fix it up on the weekends. It'll be great, you'll see. Look at all the space we're getting. There are lots of bedrooms, including one ...' he had winked at Mum, 'that would make a terrific nursery. And there's a huge garden. Not to mention quiet neighbours,' he had added with a laugh.

Mum had said, 'We did so hope you'd like it, Peter.' Her eyes had pleaded with him, like a spaniel's.

Digging his hands into his pockets, Peter had scuffed his toe in the dirt as he replied, 'Sure, I like it OK. I mean, well, yeah. It's great.'

Big ugly barn, he had thought to himself. And I guess Terry will expect me to mow that acre of lawn, too.

What was wrong with the nice little flat in Rathmines, anyway? It had always been big enough for himself and Mum . . . before. Now he was living in a big old house that made strange noises at night.

Terribly strange noises.

A second something began to gasp along with the first.

The breathing of the new one sounded as if it was being forced through a throat clogged with mucus.

'That's it,' Peter told the dark room. 'I've had enough.'

He slammed both feet down on the floor, hard. Then he fumbled in the bedside locker for the electric torch he had put there before he went to bed. This was an old house at the far end of a country lane and it was the season of summer storms. He had anticipated that the electricity might go off at any time, although he had not expected the lamp would fail to work.

As his fingers closed around the hard, smooth cylinder, he was glad he'd had the sense to plan ahead. The torch was a big one, and heavy. Slammed against an intruder's head it would make a good weapon.

Peter took a tentative step forward, his ears straining to detect the slightest change in the breathing across the room. But there was no response to his cautious advance.

He took another step.

A cold draught ran across his bare feet and ankles and sent a shiver up his spine.

Where's that coming from? he wondered.

Expecting rain, he had closed the windows before he went to bed. He looked in the direction of the door and squinted. In the gloom he could just make out the fact that it was standing ajar. Yet he was certain he had closed it. He always slept with his door closed. If the door was open, that could explain the draught.

But what opened the door?

Peter looked back towards the corner which held the mysterious breathing. The darkness seemed darker there and he could see nothing at all, not even the outline of the chair. He seemed to be looking into a yawning blackness that went on and on without end . . .

'Stop that!' Peter said aloud. He was scaring himself and he knew it. There was an electric torch in his hand; all he had to do was turn it on and shine it into the corner. He ran his thumb up the cylinder and pressed the button.

Nothing happened.

He pressed it again, harder. It was impossible that the lamp and the torch both should fail. The torch made a clicking noise but no light appeared.

If anything, the darkness facing Peter seemed to grow deeper.

There was a funny smell, too; an unpleasant tang in the air that made him feel queasy. Suddenly the last thing in the world he wanted to do was to go any further towards that lightless corner.

But what else could he do? He was equally reluctant to turn his back on . . . whatever it was, and retreat. If he did go back to bed, what then? Just lie there, waiting for whatever it was to come after him?

Or should he try to escape?

Even as the thought crossed his mind; he heard the door creak on its hinges and slam shut.

A draught could have done that, but Peter didn't think so.

Giving a cry of pure terror, he broke and ran.

Three strides carried him to the door. Dropping the torch in his haste, he caught the handle with both hands and almost wrenched it from the wood. For an awful moment he thought the door wouldn't open. Then he felt it yield.

Flinging it wide, Peter raced through and belted for the stairs.

His footsteps echoed hollowly on the wooden steps. Once he almost lost his balance and tumbled head first, but he caught hold of the banister at the last moment. He hardly slowed his pace, however. When he reached the bottom of the stairs he ran straight for the front door.

Here he stopped. And stared. 'I bolted that last thing before I went to bed,' Peter said aloud in astonishment.

Yet this door too was standing wide open.

For a moment he could not think, could not even move. Someone definitely was in the house. Intruders, burglars, or perhaps something even more sinister. Should he stay and fight? Or go for help?

He wanted to stay and fight. But only part of him wanted that; the rest of him, fortunately, was stronger. Peter plunged through the doorway and down the pathway towards the lane.

He had no real plan in mind, only an intense desire to put as much distance as possible between himself and whatever was in the corner of his bedroom. His bare feet never felt the stones in the path.

But, by the time he had gone a few hundred yards down the lane, a different sort of stone caught his attention. He was running past the old graveyard that lay beyond the house. The lopsided grin of a half-moon leered over the scene, outlining broken tombstones that emerged like rows of rotten teeth from the mossy earth. Gradually Peter slowed to a walk. His heart was still hammering, but at least he was a safe distance from the house and, as far as he could tell, nothing was chasing him.

He began to feel a little foolish again.

Maybe it had been nothing more than rats. Rats and draughts. Or even just a bad dream.

He walked on slowly, gazing towards the graveyard.

All those dead people. Lives over, futures cancelled. Nothing to look forward to any more. What would they give to be able to have a second chance, to be alive again as he was?

The worn tombstones began to have a strange effect on Peter. Instead of feeling a hushed awe, perversely he wanted to whistle and shout, laugh out loud and throw rocks and make as much noise as one boy, one living boy, possibly could. He wanted to defy death and fear and darkness. There was nothing to be scared of, just a lot of broken teeth in the moonlight.

He stopped walking and stood in the middle of the lane. 'Stupid,' he said aloud. 'Stupid, stupid, to be run out of the house like some little kid by my own imagination.'

What would Mum say? The first time he was left alone he had panicked. He had let her down, and himself as well. She and Terry had only been gone for a day and here he was practically wetting himself in the middle of the road just because he had some silly nightmare.

That's all it was. A nightmare. His warm bed was waiting for him back there, all he had to do was turn around and go home.

Home.

Lifting his chin, Peter turned around and started back towards the house. As he walked, a hundred thoughts chased themselves through his head. He'd been resenting Terry, but maybe that was a mistake. Mum was happy and they did have a home of their own now. They were going to be a family.

A real family, with a future. Husband and wife and son, and maybe a baby sometime. A little sister, he'd like that.

And to think he had almost ruined it. What was the last thing he had said to Terry as they left that morning?

'Don't hurry back,' Peter had hissed under his breath so low that only Mum's new husband could hear. Then the car door slammed and, as it drove off, he had stood in front of the house, waving, and saying aloud although Terry could no longer hear him, 'You don't have to come back at all as far as I'm concerned.'

He had meant it just then. But he didn't mean it now.

He was so preoccupied he did not hear the car drive up behind him until a man's voice called gently, 'Are you all right, son?'

Peter whirled around, half expecting to find Terry sitting in the car and grinning out at him. But it wasn't Terry. It was a police car with two strange men in it. One of them got out and came towards him.

'Are you Peter Ryan?'

'I am.'

'Perhaps we'd better go inside, son. We have some news for you.'

The man's voice was so gentle that Peter knew at once. He would do anything to keep from hearing what they had come to say, but the two policemen took him inside and turned on the lights and sat him down on a chair in the parlour. Then they told him. Accident . . . car crash . . . both killed instantly . . . so terribly sorry . . .

As if through a roaring fog Peter heard, not the policeman's words, but the very last thing his mother had said to him. He'd been wrong, it wasn't, 'You will be all right, Peter, won't you?'

Just before the car that would kill them drove away, she had leaned towards him with that radiant, happy smile, and said, 'We'll come back to you, Peter, I promise. We'll always come back to you.'

With dawning horror Peter looked past the policemen towards the stairs. And his bedroom. And whatever waited in the corner.

The Front Room

MICHELLE MAGORIAN

Helen woke up sharply. Face to the wall, she felt again that horrifying presence behind her. She took a deep breath, gritted her teeth, and forced herself to look round. In the semi-darkness shadows moved. She pushed herself quickly out of bed, sprinted across the room and turned on the light.

All she could see was her bed up by the window, a faded sofa, two armchairs, a shabby carpet, and a table and two chairs up against the wall by the door. Even so, she decided to keep the light on. Her parents would be furious if she woke them up a fourth night running. When she had dashed into their room the previous night, their patience had finally snapped.

'There's absolutely nothing wrong with that room,' her mother had said. 'You're acting like a baby. Anybody would think you were two instead of eleven.'

'You know your mother needs a good rest,' said her father. 'If I have any more of this nonsense, I'll stop your pocket money.'

Helen had clambered quickly back into bed. She needed that pocket money desperately. For over a year she had been saving up for a guitar. Her father had even promised that if she helped out and did some baby-sitting he'd pay her proper baby-sitting rates as well.

'Couldn't I sleep with Brian?' she had suggested.

Her three-year-old brother slept at the end of the corridor in a small room which led into the kitchen.

'There's not enough room,' her mother had said crossly. 'It's only a divan.'

'But, Mum—' Helen had protested.

'Now belt up,' her father had said, 'or I'll give you a good hiding.'

Her parents weren't usually so bad-tempered, but ever since Mum had lost the baby they always seemed to be quarrelling.

Helen pulled the curtains aside and stared out at the dark street below. They had been lucky to find this holiday flat at all, and the old woman who owned the place had gone out of her way to put a bed into the front room for Helen.

As soon as the dawn came, Helen felt it was safe enough to go back to sleep. She had hardly closed her eyes when she was being woken up by her father.

'Did you sleep with the light on all night?' he said angrily.

'No, Dad, only a bit of it. I didn't want to wake you up.'

Her father sat on the bed. He was a big man with a round nose and untidy brown hair. Helen, though small, was the spitting image of him.

'Look, kiddo.' He always called her that when he treated her special. 'What's up?'

She pushed herself up onto her elbows. 'I don't know. One minute I'm asleep and then I wake up and I can feel someone in the room.'

Her father gazed awkwardly at his hands. 'Look,' he said, 'I know me and your mum haven't been getting on too well lately. That's because we're tired and we're a bit upset because of the baby. You know.'

'Yeah.'

'We're just going through a bad patch, that's all. Your mum's already looking a bit perkier. The sea air's cheering her up. I know it's not much of a holiday for you, but if you could just keep on looking after Brian, it'd make a lot of difference.'

Helen sat up, puzzled. 'But you know I'm happy to do that, Dad.'

And it was true. Looking after Brian, so that her parents could go off together, made her feel useful, important.

'I thought maybe you were a bit fed up of being left with him and were trying to get your own back.'

'Dad!'

'I just wanted to make sure,' he said, standing up. 'I'll get breakfast going, eh?' And he gave a broad grin.

Helen grinned back and pushed the bedclothes aside.

Her first job in the morning was to wash and dress Brian. Mum had breakfast in bed on a tray. Dad had refused to let her get up for breakfast all through the holiday. That morning she and Brian stuck a little bunch of flowers in an empty fish-paste pot filled with water, and her father placed it on the tray and carried it in to her mother. After eating breakfast with them, he took a mug of tea into the bedroom while Helen washed up.

Brian stood on the chair by the sink, pretending to be useful but really making a lot of mess on the floor. Helen put her arm round him and pressed her cheek against his.

'Now,' she said, 'you can help me make the sandwiches.'

'Want a rorange juice,' he demanded.

She was in the middle of pasting strawberry jam on some bread when she heard her parents walking through the little room where Brian slept. As soon as her mother opened the kitchen door, Helen looked anxiously up at her, and then immediately felt relieved. The grey shadows under her eyes had at last begun to disappear and she actually had some colour in her cheeks. She was wearing her pink cotton dressing gown, her long black hair scooped back untidily from her face.

'You're looking very peaky, Helen,' she said. 'You didn't have another bad dream, did you?'

'Too much reading,' her father said quickly.

'Yeah,' said Helen. 'I got this smashing book. I couldn't put it down last night.'

Helen finished making the sandwiches and then began to

collect towels and buckets. Brian trailed after her as she walked through his room, down the long narrow passage and up to the door of the front room. She pushed it open. Her duffle-bag was hanging from the back of a chair over by the table.

'Want a rorange juice,' Brian said impatiently.

'In a minute.'

Brian scowled and sat down in the corridor, tracing the patterns on the faded lino with his fingers.

Helen picked up a towel and swimsuit and shoved them into the bag. She slung it over her shoulder and then leaned out of the window. The sea was only five minutes walk away.

Suddenly she felt a cold tingling sensation moving slowly down the back of her neck, right to the base of her spine. She whirled round but again she could see nothing. It was almost as if whatever it was slipped behind her back every time she moved. She pressed herself against the wall. Without thinking, her hand automatically went up to her throat as if to protect it. She pushed herself away.

'Come on, Brian,' she said.

She wanted to run, but instead she forced herself to move casually, so as not to alarm him.

It wasn't until later that evening, in a pub down by the harbour, that Helen raised the subject of the room. The pub had a section for families, where they could sit and look out at all the boats coming in to moor. As soon as her mother had nipped off to the loo, Helen grabbed her chance.

'Dad,' she said quickly, 'could we change where my bed is and put it by the opposite wall?'

'Now don't you start on about that room again,' he warned.

'I just want the bed moved, that's all. I think it's the rattling of the windows that's scaring me.'

He smiled. 'Piece of cake, kiddo. We'll shift it as soon as we get back.'

Helen could have wept with relief. At least she'd feel a bit safer up by the wall of her parents' bedroom *and* she'd be nearer the light switch.

As soon as they returned, she and her father moved the bed. Her mother was all for it, too. 'I thought she was catching a bit of a chill by that window,' she remarked. Helen's father winked at her.

After Brian had gone to bed, Helen and her parents played Monopoly. She didn't care for the game much. It was too slow. Monotony, she called it. But it was different that night. Her mother was smiling. So was her dad. When it was time to go to bed, the last sound Helen heard before falling asleep was her parents chatting over a game of cards.

At first she thought it was the sound of her own breathing that had woken her, but she realized only too quickly that the breathing was coming from someone else. It was a rasping, asthmatic sort of breath. She sat up slowly and peered into the darkness.

A floorboard creaked. It came from the direction of the window. It was followed immediately by another creak. There was no mistaking it: someone was in the room. She listened, terrified, as the creaking grew louder and nearer, and the breathing turned into loud heaving gasps.

Helen jumped out of bed, turned on the light and hastily looked round the room. There was no one there. Still frightened, she backed out of the door. She would spend the rest of the night in the kitchen.

The dawn was a long time coming. Even when it was light, Helen had no idea of the time. She pressed her ear up against the transistor radio, keeping the volume low. Anything to hear the comforting sound of a voice. At eight o'clock, she turned the sound up and began to lay the table. She was just pouring the milk into a jug, when the door knob moved. She jumped. Brian opened the door, his eyes sticky with sleep.

'Oh, Brian,' Helen said, picking him up and giving him a squeeze. 'I'm so glad to see you.'

'Want a rorange juice,' he said, rubbing his eyes.

As she sat him down, her parents walked in, still in their nightclothes. 'Hello, Dad,' she said brightly. 'Thought I'd give you a surprise breakfast. I'll put the kettle on.'

Her father eyed her suspiciously. 'I didn't hear you get up.'

'You ought to go back to bed,' said her mother. 'You look awful.'

'I'm all right.'

''Course she is,' said her father abruptly. 'Come on, let's get breakfast started.'

Helen knew that she had to get her father on his own but it wasn't until the afternoon that her chance came. They were walking back to the flat after lunch in a café on the seafront. It was raining and her mother and Brian had rushed on ahead.

Helen grabbed her father by the arm. 'Dad, I've got to tell you about last night!'

'I know about last night,' he said. 'You had another of your nightmares, I suppose.'

They had stopped in a doorway to watch the wind whipping rain along the quay. People in summer clothes ran for shelter, holding newspapers over their heads.

'Please, Dad,' Helen said. 'I heard footsteps and this horrible breathing.'

He turned sharply to look at her. 'What?'

'Honest, Dad. It was over by the window. I thought it was a nightmare but I sat right up in bed and the sounds got louder and started to come towards me.'

Her father started to walk on. Helen had to run to keep up with him. 'But when I turned the light on,' she continued, 'there was no one there.'

'Well, there you are then,' he said. 'It must have been a bad dream.'

Helen turned crossly away. 'You don't believe me, do you?' She shoved her hands in the pockets of her jeans.

'Look, kiddo,' he began.

'Don't call me kiddo!'

'Well, you're acting like a kid!' he said angrily. 'These stupid nightmares!'

'They're *not* nightmares!' Helen yelled. 'I've told you I'm awake when it happens.' She strode briskly on ahead, swallowing her tears and rage. One minute adults expected you to be grown-up, but if you tried to talk to them they refused to listen. If a grown-up had told him the story, he'd have listened all right.

Her father caught up with her and pulled her under his umbrella. He drew her close to him and gave her a hug. Before she could stop herself, Helen burst into tears. She was so tired. She'd give anything for a good night's sleep.

'Look,' her father said quietly, 'we've only got a few nights left.'

'I know, Dad, but I can't sleep in there again, I just can't.'

He took out a handkerchief and wiped her face. 'Don't worry, we'll sort something out.'

Later, in the kitchen, when Brian was asleep and her mother had gone into the bedroom to put on some make-up, Helen's father took her to one side.

'Are you sure you'll be all right on your own?' he asked.

Helen nodded.

'We'll be at the pub down by the harbour. We'll only be gone an hour.'

'Don't worry, Dad. Stay longer if you want. I'll sit here in the kitchen.'

'We'll come straight back. You look like you could do with an early night.' He paused. 'I still don't know where we're going to put you.'

'I'll make up a bed in the bath,' she said, grinning.

He ruffled her hair. 'Attagirl.'

After her parents had left, Helen settled down at the kitchen table to read her book. It wasn't until later that she ventured into the front room. She had started to scribble down some verses for a song and had run out of paper. She knew that there was an exercise book on the table in her room.

'Oh, come on,' she whispered to herself. 'It's only a stupid room, and it isn't even dark yet.'

As soon as she entered the room she sensed that the evil that had been there had finally disappeared. It was as if it had been swept away by a mysterious force. She didn't feel scared any more. Relieved, she shut the door behind her, picked up the exercise book and sat down on the bed. She had thought of a word to rhyme with 'trail' and wanted to write it down immediately in case she forgot it. 'Hail,' she scribbled.

It was so cosy and comfortable in the room that she stayed there, writing busily. As she was racking her brain for a word to rhyme with 'saddle', her eyelids began to flicker. Gradually her head sank heavily onto the page and the pencil slipped from her fingers.

She had no idea what time it was when she woke. She only knew that it was dark. Light from the street outside spilled eerily across the carpet. She gripped the eiderdown, terrified, and struggled to shake off her fear but it was no good. She knew that something had woken her, and that it was still somewhere

in the room. She turned her head slowly, taking in the tiled fireplace, the corner where an old gramophone stood near a handful of books on a shelf, past the window with its fluttering curtains, and along the wall to the table.

And then she saw him. A tall man standing in the shadows. He had dark, straggly hair and a black beard. His arms hung by his sides, motionless.

Helen quickly turned her head away. It's a nightmare, she thought. I'm dreaming that I've woken up. She squeezed her eyes shut. Suddenly, there was a slight movement by the bed. She opened her eyes. The man was towering above her. I'm dreaming this, she thought. I'm dreaming, I'm dreaming, I'm dreaming. The figure leaned towards her. Please let me wake up soon. But the large shadow loomed nearer and she felt his hands grip her violently round the throat.

With one enormous effort she struggled free, and scrambled backwards, half-stumbling, half-falling over the back of the bed. Petrified she switched the light on. The room was empty.

She opened the door and padded swiftly and

silently through Brian's room into the kitchen. Once there, she felt safe. She slid the window up and leaned out, gasping. She shivered and looked round for a sweater. It was then that she caught sight of her reflection in the small cracked mirror above the sink. She gave a startled cry, for there on her neck were the red marks made by the man's hands. She hadn't imagined him, after all.

She flung open the door into her brother's room, ran in, and dragged him out of bed.

Helen stood outside the pub by the harbour. Rain was lashing her face mercilessly, and her arms were aching from the effort of carrying Brian. He began to cry. She unzipped her sodden anorak and wrapped it round him. Then she found a door and slipped inside. A group of people were sitting on red plastic seats. A man behind the bar caught sight of her at once. ''Ere,' he said firmly. 'Outside!'

'I'm looking for me mum and dad,' said Helen. 'It's urgent.'

'Anyone own these two?' the man yelled.

Helen felt her face grow red as everyone turned to look at her. 'You'd best go home,' the man said.

Outside, the sea was hurling itself against the harbour wall. Helen could hardly see for the spray in her eyes. There was another pub in the distance. Still carrying Brian, she lowered her head and pushed against the swirl of wind.

After half an hour she had run out of pubs. Exhausted, she stumbled back along the beach and into a shelter where there were some wooden seats. Brian began to shiver. She was just rubbing his hands when she heard heavy footsteps approaching. She froze for an instant, and then she picked Brian up again, shot out of the shelter and ran. The footsteps quickened. Suddenly she was gripped from behind and twisted round. She peered up, terrified. It was a policeman.

He wouldn't listen to her either. All he said was something about getting dry and looking after the little chap and finding her parents. Even when they were both sitting in the warmth of the police station, with mugs of tea in their hands, the policeman just kept shaking his head and muttering, 'Kids!' It was only when Helen gave him her address that he began to look interested.

'It's in St Andrew's Road,' she said.

The sergeant, who had been standing with his back to them, swung round, startled. 'St Andrew's, did you say? A top floor flat?'

Helen nodded.

'And you say that you think a man was trying to kill you?'

'Yes, but when I turned on the light he wasn't there.'

'It wouldn't be number forty-three, would it?' the sergeant asked gently.

'Yes, that's right.'

'Woodfield,' he said to the young constable, 'see if a Mr and Mrs Robinson are in the top flat at number forty-three.'

'But they might not be there,' Helen blurted out. 'And if they aren't, I couldn't go back there on my own.'

'Don't worry, girl, you won't have to.'

Helen leaned back in relief, and sipped her tea. Brian was curled up on the bench beside her, half asleep.

Shortly after that, two policemen returned with her parents. Her mum was in a terrible state; her dad, furious.

'Where the hell have you been?' he yelled. 'Me and your mum have been worried sick.'

'Mr Robinson,' said the sergeant firmly. 'I'd like to speak to you and your wife in private.'

'We only left them for an hour—' her father began.

'Please,' said the sergeant.

Helen watched as they went into an adjoining room. She did her best to eavesdrop from the bench but the two policemen in charge cottoned on, and started to talk loudly about some football match. When her parents reappeared, they looked stunned. Her father glanced across at her strangely.

'What's the matter, Dad?'

'Come on,' he said. 'We're going to move into a bed-and-breakfast.'

From then on, it was all a blur. All Helen could remember was a trip up a heavily carpeted staircase, and sitting in a warm bath, and being wrapped up in a towel by her father.

When she awoke the next morning, she found that she was lying in a small bed with a pink bedspread on it. Her mother was sitting at a dressing table, writing postcards.

'What time is it?' said Helen.

Her mother turned and smiled. 'Eleven o'clock. You've been asleep for twelve hours.' She came and sat on the bed and smoothed Helen's fringe gently behind her ears. 'Hurry up and get dressed. We'll go down to that fisherman's caff by the harbour and have a big fry-up.'

It wasn't until Helen had tucked into egg, bacon, fried bread, tomatoes, sausages, and two large mugs of tea that her mother answered her questions about the flat.

'Are you sure you want to know?' she asked.

'Oh, Mum!' said Helen impatiently. ''Course I do.'

'Well,' began her mother, 'twenty-five years ago, a man murdered three children in that front room.'

'Blimey!' whispered Helen.

'And they were all girls.'

'They were strangled, weren't they?' said Helen quietly.

Her mother nodded.

Helen suddenly felt very cold. 'But is the man still alive, or what?'

'He was hanged.'

'But I felt his hands.' She looked hard at her mother. 'Honest, Mum, I really did.'

'Look, love, I believe you. I wish I'd known. I'd never have let you sleep in there.' She gave a shudder. 'Anyway, that's all over now. We'll have a lovely day together and stay at the bed-and-breakfast from now on.'

Helen gave a relieved sigh and gazed at the heavy drizzle which had begun to fall outside.

Suddenly she felt a hand on her shoulder. She gave a startled yell and whirled round. It was her father.

'Dad!' she cried. 'Don't do that! You scared me!'

'Sorry,' he said sheepishly. Both his hands were now firmly held behind his back.

'Dad!' Helen said suspiciously. 'What are you hiding?'

Slowly he revealed a large wooden object which he placed in her lap.

'A guitar!' she exclaimed.

It was a Spanish one. Just like a real folk singer's. She let her hands glide slowly over the wooden curves.

'I bought it at a second-hand shop round the corner,' her father said. 'I'm afraid it's a bit damp from the rain, though.'

He took out a handkerchief and began to wipe it down.

'Oh, Dad,' Helen whispered, and beamed at him.

Within minutes, her head was bowed over the guitar and her thumb and fingers were plucking the strings. Gradually her parents' voices faded into the distance. She didn't even hear her brother asking for more orange juice, or the sound of the rain growing heavier. She had quite forgotten that she was sitting in a caff down by the harbour. And the murderous ghost? She had forgotten him, too.

Dream Justice

E. W. MAYO

The strange circumstances surrounding the death of Edward Martin were never fully revealed to the public. It was thought by most people that he died of causes unknown, even to the doctors.

But the following I found in his diary; and although there is no way of proving the truth or untruth of it, I nevertheless am inclined to think it explains his death more satisfactorily than any other reason given:

Feb. 7—Last night I had a dream—a dream that was only too true. I dreamed that a murder I had committed three years ago, which I thought had been successfully covered up, had been brought to light. The evidence against me was so forceful that I confessed. I was then taken to the county jail, where I was charged with murder in the first degree. At this point I awoke and found myself wet with perspiration. Why, although the facts concerning the murder are true, I should have a dream of this sort, I can't explain.

Feb. 8—My dream was continued last night. This time it seemed to cover a period of some weeks. I was convicted and sentenced to die in the electric chair on August 20. After my sentence was passed I again awoke to find myself in a cold sweat. I was extremely nervous today and am hoping I won't have another of these foolish dreams. The murder is completely covered up, I'm sure, and I was never suspected, so there is no need to be afraid or worried even if I do dream of it. But still I would like an explanation for it.

Feb. 9—It was awful last night. Time passed quickly and it was only three days before the day set for my electrocution when I awoke. It really seemed as if I had spent those long weeks in my cell, waiting and waiting. Today I was really worried, and my friends wanted to know what was wrong with me.

Feb. 10—Two more days—and then—? I can't get away from it, I dream and dream—it is terrible. I even plotted an escape from prison last night—but failed. The thing preys on my mind all the time now—day and night. I can't eat, I can't do anything —I look and act insane; my friends demand to know what the trouble is—but I don't dare tell them—they couldn't help me. No one can help me—if only I could get away from those cursed, those infernal dreams!

Feb. 11—One more day. Last night was a repetition of the one before. I didn't go out today—I was afraid my friends might hear me talking and muttering to myself. I seem to be out of my head—I feel weak and can hardly think at all. I only dread what tonight will bring.

Feb. 12—Tonight at 12—I'm doomed to go then. But I think I have a way to fool them—I won't go to sleep—I'll stay up and awake until after 12—maybe that will end it all—maybe the spell will be broken then and I shall be saved. I'll drink coffee—black coffee—lots of it—that will keep me awake.

10 p.m.—So far I've been able to keep awake—but I'm getting a little drowsy—I guess I need more black coffee.

11 p.m.—I'm so tired and sleepy I can hardly hold my head up—maybe I need a little fresh air—going to open a window. Just another hour or more and then—if I can only hold out till then!

11:55 p.m.—I can barely write—I almost went under that time —a few more minutes—I can't—I can't—my eyes—I can't hold them open—I'm going—I'm going—

Such were the contents of the late Edward Martin's diary.

And what was found when his bedroom door was forced?

His dead body, slumped down in a big armchair, with peculiar marks on his wrists and ankles—marks that weren't explained at that time—or ever.

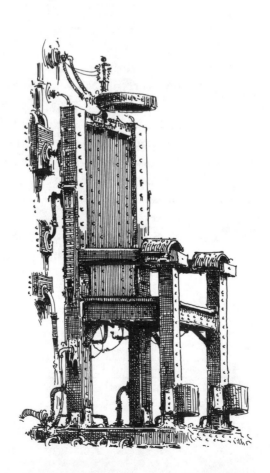

The Patch

PHILIP MURRAY

I think you'll be comfortable here,' said my hostess. 'Of course the panelling and the old four-poster make the room look rather gloomy, but with that huge fire and plenty of candles you'll be quite snug and cheery.'

'It's delightful,' I replied; 'I love old rooms like this, with mullioned windows, open fireplaces, and ancient furniture. Are there any secret cupboards or hidden doors?'

'I'm sure I don't know,' she laughed. 'I don't think we've ever taken the trouble to explore this part of the house. It's such a rambling old place. But I mustn't keep you; dinner at eight sharp, and Harry's fearfully punctual. I'll send my maid to fasten your dress.'

A long train journey, a drive of six miles in a dog-cart and a huge dinner in a well-warmed room combined to make my eyelids weary before the clock struck ten, and it was not many minutes after I regained my room that I was clambering into the old four-poster.

The firelight glancing from the polished surface of the panelling and lighting up the heavy velvet-covered furniture kept me awake for a little time, and I mused on those who might have occupied the rooms since the old house was built. Pondering thus I fell asleep.

I awoke suddenly, conscious that something had touched me, and instinctively I became aware that there was someone under the bed. The fire had died down to a dull glow, giving the room an unearthly appearance.

For a moment I was panic-stricken and paralysed, and amid my terror I could feel the sweat forming and running off my forehead. Then I collected my senses and blamed myself for having omitted to place candle and matches by my bedside. I listened: the silence was profound.

Then came another moment of terror: I had forgotten where the door was, and in the gloom the panelling seemed continuous round the room. I waited, stiff with fright, wondering from which side of the bed *it* would emerge. If only something would make a noise!

At last I decided to make a spring for the fireplace and snatch up the poker. At least I could keep the intruder off whilst I screamed for help. But I found that I could not move, and one cannot spring out over the foot of a bed from the sitting-up position. It was some minutes before I could force my muscles to act, then I reached the fireplace in one scrambling bound, snatched up the poker and faced about.

Perfect silence.

After a minute or so I managed to light the candles within reach. Still no sound. Growing bolder I tiptoed towards the door; reached it; opened it. Silence still. There was a light in the passage, and then I heard voices in a neighbouring room. Courage returned; I stooped down and looked under the bed.

A man was lying there on his side, his face towards me, his knees drawn up.

I slammed the door and flew towards the voices.

When my fellow guests accompanied me back a few minutes later and threw open the door the room was as I had left it.

They stooped down and looked under the bed, rising quickly. 'He's there all right,' said one. 'Out you come.' Silence. He stooped down again and thrust his poker at the man. The poker met with no obstruction.

'Good God,' he cried, 'what is it?'

They both knelt and peered under the bed. Presently one gave a laugh—rather a nervous laugh, but a laugh.

'Why,' he said, 'it's not a man at all; it's a stain or patch on the carpet. Look; I can put my poker through it.'

By the light of more candles we saw that he was right. It was a dark patch, caused apparently by a stain of some sort, and it had exactly the appearance I have described.

I duly returned to bed, and at last fell asleep; but my nerves were shattered, and nightmare succeeded nightmare.

Next morning there was a full inspection. Daylight dissipated all fears, and I pooh-poohed the idea of moving to another room. 'Anyway,' said my hostess, 'the bed shall be moved to the other side of the room. I'll get some of the men to do it before lunch.'

But when the bed was moved the patch seemed to have disappeared. At least, only the pattern of the carpet in that particular spot could account for a very far-fetched resemblance to a man.

Still, when I entered my bedroom that night I felt glad that the change had been made. It was rather odd altogether, and my dreams too . . . It was just as well the bed had been moved. I undressed and climbed leisurely into it. Then I paused. 'Tonight I'll make sure there's nothing under it.' I stooped down and looked under the bed.

A man was lying there on his side, his face towards me, his knees drawn up.

The Eyes

KIT PEARSON

I don't like her eyes,' said Bernie. She pointed to one of
the six dolls sitting on a shelf in her aunt's guest bedroom.

'That one?' said Aunt Sheila. She laughed. 'I don't blame
you. I never have either.'

Michelle picked up the doll, straightened her green plaid
skirt, and pushed her hair back under her bonnet. 'What's
wrong with her? She's pretty?'

Bernie stared at the doll's face. Her porcelain cheeks were
tinted pink and her mouth curved into a half-smile. Michelle
took her finger and rubbed dust out of the doll's eyes. They
were a peculiar yellow-orange, like a cat's eyes, veined with
black and fringed all around with delicately painted lashes. The
eyes seemed to be watching Bernie.

'She's very pretty,' Aunt Sheila agreed. 'The prettiest of all
my childhood dolls. But I never played with her, partly because

she's so fragile. That's why she's in such good condition.' She put the doll back on the shelf. 'You're both welcome to play with any of these, though.'

Bernie looked longingly at the other five dolls, but Michelle said, 'We're too old for dolls.'

'Shall I leave the hall light on for you?' Aunt Sheila asked.

'No thanks,' said Michelle. 'Bernie and I *like* the dark, right?'

'Uh huh,' Bernie gulped.

'Goodnight then, girls. Sleep as long as you want in the morning. I'm so glad to have you here at last.' Aunt Sheila kissed them both and went downstairs.

Michelle was silent almost immediately, but Bernie couldn't sink into the sleep her exhausted body craved. It had been such a long day, flying clear across Canada to this large city on the west coast.

She and Michelle were spending the last three weeks of the summer vacation with Aunt Sheila, their father's sister. They saw her every Christmas in Nova Scotia when she visited her parents. She was their favourite aunt, and she had been so excited when Bernie and Michelle had finally accepted her yearly invitation to visit.

They hadn't come before because of Bernie. She was afraid of flying, even with her older sister along. And Michelle wasn't allowed to go alone—their parents said it wasn't fair. 'You're such a coward!' she hissed at Bernie every year when she'd refused.

This year Dad had sat Bernie down after her tenth birthday and thought he'd persuaded her to do it. But it was Michelle's disdain that Bernie couldn't stand any longer.

Michelle was only a year older than Bernie, but she was trying to grow up as fast as she could. She had all sorts of standards. Saying 'Dad' instead of 'Daddy'; not playing with dolls after the age of eight; getting your ears pierced at ten. Bernie had been relieved when their parents extended this to twelve; *she* didn't want holes poked in her ears.

Bernie tried her best to live up to her sister's expectations, but she was afraid of so many things that it was often difficult. The plane trip had been awful. Her body was still taut with the fear she'd struggled with the whole time. It didn't matter how kind the flight attendant had been or how nice Michelle was to her on the plane. She couldn't eat, and when they arrived her legs wouldn't work properly.

'See?' Michelle said as they walked into the airport. 'I told you it would be easy.'

Only Aunt Sheila understood. 'Was it terrible, poor Bernie?' she whispered through her hug. 'I'm so proud of you. It's very brave to make yourself do something that frightens you so much.'

And now here they were, safe in Aunt Sheila's house in Vancouver. It was close to the beach and they were going there first thing tomorrow. Aunt Sheila had taken time off work and she had lots of treats planned for them—a trip to Victoria on the ferry, to a water park, to movies and the rides at the exhibition. And in the third week Mum and Dad were flying out to join them.

Bernie hunched further under the quilt. She should be ready to sleep off her ordeal. So why was she still so tense?

Because the room was so dark; at home the hall light *was* left on.

It was silly to feel scared. If she'd conquered the plane, she should be able to face the dark. She pulled the quilt off her face and turned over on to her back. High on the shelf opposite the bed, the doll's eyes glittered—two yellow orbs in the blackness, staring straight at Bernie.

Bernie shrieked, but no sound came. She hid her head, then glanced out again. The eyes still shone and their pupils swelled and shrank like those in real eyes.

'Michelle!' Bernie squealed, leaping to her sister's bed and shaking her.

Michelle thrashed and groaned. 'Leave me *alone*, I'm asleep!'

'Michelle, p-please . . .' Bernie crawled into bed beside her sister and whispered into her ear. 'That d-doll—her eyes are—they're alive! They're shining! Look!'

'You are such an idiot . . . ' Michelle sat up briefly, glanced at the doll, and flopped down. 'They are *not*, Bernie. Get back into your own bed and let me sleep!'

Bernie made herself look again. 'They *are!*'

But Michelle pushed Bernie on to the floor, turned her back on her, and didn't move.

Bernie jumped back under her own covers. She curled up in the hot cave, breathing hard.

Was she dreaming? She risked one more peek, then dived under again. The flickering eyes were even brighter. They burned into Bernie's own eyes.

Bernie clutched her knees to her chest and stayed that way until her body finally collapsed into sleep.

'Weren't you hot, sleeping under the covers all night?'

Bernie's head emerged. Michelle was her usual busy morning self. She rushed to the window. 'It's a great day for the beach! Let's put our bathing suits on under our shorts.'

But Bernie stayed in bed, rigidly not looking at the shelf.

'Bernie! What's the matter, are you sick?'

'That doll,' Bernie whispered. 'She was staring at me all night. I could feel her eyes, even though I hid under the quilt. I could feel her staring even when I was asleep.'

Michelle was pulling off her pyjamas. 'Honestly, Bernie. It was a *dream*. You were probably dreaming about that video we rented about a doll that came alive.'

'I didn't watch that,' Bernie said, shuddering.

'Well, it must have been a dream. She's just a doll—look and you'll see.'

Taking a deep breath, Bernie sat up and turned her head towards the doll.

Michelle was right—she was just a doll. She gazed blankly into the air the way the other dolls did, not at Bernie. Her yellow eyes glinted a bit in the sunlight, but they were just glass, not alive.

'Maybe it *was* a dream,' Bernie said slowly.

'Of course it was. Come on, let's go and wake up Aunt Sheila.'

That night Bernie considered asking Aunt Sheila to put the doll somewhere else. But now that she felt relaxed she was more and more convinced that the gleaming eyes had been only a dream.

They'd had a wonderful day. The Pacific Ocean was much warmer than the Atlantic. They had swum and built castles with moats that filled up when the tide came in. They had lunch at a hamburger stand and went to Stanley Park in the afternoon.

Bernie and Michelle lay in bed and chatted drowsily until Michelle's last sentence dwindled away. Bernie fell asleep soon after.

A few hours later she shuddered violently, turned over, and woke up. Someone was looking at her. She *knew* it. Whoever it was was forcing her to open her eyes and look back.

The amber eyes floated in the darkness as if they weren't connected to a face. They seemed even more full of menace than last night.

Bernie stumbled out of the room and down the stairs. She crawled into bed with Aunt Sheila.

'What's the matter, Bernie? You're shaking!'

'The eyes—the *eyes* . . .' Bernie sobbed.

Aunt Sheila drew her close and tucked her blanket around both of them. 'It's all right, sweetheart. You've had a nightmare. Go back to sleep—you're safe now.'

'Aunt Sheila, please take that doll out of our room,' Bernie said at breakfast.

'What a baby!' Michelle scoffed. 'Do you still think it's looking at you?'

'Yes,' Bernie whispered.

'Leave her alone, Michelle.' Aunt Sheila patted Bernie's shoulder. 'If the doll bothers you, of course I'll take it away.'

Bernie wouldn't go into the bedroom until Aunt Sheila had carried the doll down to the basement. She watched from the top of the stairs as her aunt wrapped the doll in an old towel, put her into a cardboard box, and closed the flaps.

'There!' Aunt Sheila looked up at Bernie. 'She can stay in this box until you leave, all right?'

Bernie wasn't sure if it was all right. The doll was out of sight, but her fiery eyes were still in Bernie's mind.

She tried to think of other things. Their cousin Jennifer came over, and Bernie and Michelle were surprised that Jennifer, at thirteen, suggested playing with Aunt Sheila's dolls.

'Of course I'm too old for this,' she said, taking a tiny leather boot out of the bag of dolls' clothes. 'But isn't it neat how Aunt Sheila has kept these? I've played with them all my life. But where's the other one—the fancy one with the china face?'

Please don't tell her, Bernie begged Michelle silently.

Luckily Michelle didn't seem to want to admit that her sister was a coward. 'What other one?' she asked innocently.

'There's one more doll. Maybe Aunt Sheila put her away so you wouldn't break her. She has a funny name—Grizel!'

Michelle giggled. 'Grizel?'

'Isn't it weird? She came from Scotland—she belonged to our great-grandmother, the one who came to Canada with her husband.' Jennifer finished tying the tiny bootlaces and looked up. 'Do you want to see her?'

'See who?' Bernie whispered.

'Grizel! I'm sure Aunt Sheila would show her to you.'

Michelle looked at Bernie. 'No, thanks. Bernie and I are too old for dolls. Come on, it must be time to go to the movie.'

Bernie tried to lose herself in the movie, but she couldn't help thinking of Grizel. Now that she knew her name, the doll felt even more alive. It suited her—an ugly name for something ugly that stared out of the doll's pretty face.

She remembered what Dad had said when he talked to her about flying. 'If you're scared of something, find out more about it.' He had shown her statistics about how safe flying was. It hadn't helped—Bernie had still spent the whole time thinking the plane was going to crash. But maybe it would help with Grizel. She had to do something to get the image of the doll's burning eyes out of her head.

That evening she helped her aunt load the dishwasher while Michelle and Jennifer watched TV. 'Aunt Sheila,' she began carefully, 'could you tell me more about that doll I don't like? Jennifer said her name was Grizel and that she belonged to our great-grandmother.'

'I . . . suppose I could. First let me make some tea.'

Bernie watched her aunt pour boiling water into the teapot and get out the cups. She poured Bernie tea with lots of milk in it, and they sat down at the kitchen table.

Why did Aunt Sheila seem so reluctant to speak? 'It's OK,' Bernie said. 'I don't really want to know any more about the doll.'

Aunt Sheila stirred her tea. 'No, I'm glad you asked. You girls *should* know, Bernie. Maybe you especially.'

'Why?'

'Because you're so imaginative and sensitive. Like Grizel's owner—your great-grandmother Margaret. You even look a bit like her.'

'Did you ever meet her?'

Aunt Sheila nodded. 'I knew her all my childhood, although no one knew her well. She was a very reserved woman and she always looked sad. But one day towards the end of her life she told me a tragic story. I was only sixteen, but I've never forgotten it.' Aunt Sheila put a hand on top of Bernie's. 'Shall I tell you? I don't want to give you nightmares again.'

Bernie swallowed hard. 'Tell me.'

'It was about a fire,' Aunt Sheila began slowly. Bernie's insides quaked. One of her night-time fears was of a fire breaking out while she was asleep.

'Grannie grew up on the east coast of Scotland. She had two older sisters and a younger brother—his name was Ewan, and she adored him. She used to pull him around the town streets in a wagon, and they shared a room. The other thing she adored was her doll.'

'Grizel,' Bernie breathed.

'Yes, a funny name to us but a common one in Scotland then. It's short for Grizelda. Margaret was given Grizel for her eighth birthday, and she took her everywhere for the next four years. Girls grew up more slowly then, it wasn't unusual for a twelve year old to play with dolls. Margaret and Ewan were constantly making up stories about Grizel, how she was really a princess and lived in a land called . . . Ilore or something. I know: Eleuria.'

Bernie smiled; sometimes, when she couldn't sleep, she made up an imaginary land. 'Did she tell you much about Eleuria?'

'Not really—she was a bit embarrassed about it, but it was obvious she remembered a lot of what they pretended. She said that she and Ewan talked about Eleuria all the time. They used to carry Grizel around on a red cushion, and Margaret sewed royal clothes for her.'

Bernie thought of Grizel's terrifying eyes—obviously they hadn't bothered these two long-ago children.

'One evening Margaret's parents and older sisters went to a lecture. They left Margaret in charge of Ewan. She was twelve and he was six. They trusted her to take good care of the brother she loved so much. They weren't going to be late.'

Aunt Sheila sighed, took a deep drink of tea, and continued. 'They didn't have electricity in their house—they used paraffin lamps. Margaret and Ewan propped up Grizel on a high shelf and pretended to be courtiers bringing her presents. They draped themselves in shawls and began dancing for Grizel. Then Margaret had to go to the outside toilet. She said Ewan was still whirling around when she left. The edge of his shawl must have knocked over a lamp. Margaret heard him scream and ran back into the house, but she was overcome by smoke and fainted outside the room.'

Bernie gasped, and Aunt Sheila put an arm around her shoulder as she continued. 'Her family arrived home just in time to drag her to safety. But it was too late for Ewan—he was burned to death.'

Neither of them spoke for a minute. Finally Bernie whispered, 'What about Grizel?'

'Grannie said she wasn't damaged at all. When the fire brigade arrived she got soaked with water and she smelled of smoke for months afterwards—but she was sitting up so high she escaped the flames.'

Aunt Sheila sighed, 'I don't think Grannie ever got over it. She blamed herself for Ewan's death—that's why she always looked so sad.'

She paused, looking sad herself.

'There's more, isn't there?' Bernie whispered.

'Yes . . . Grannie said that from then on Grizel changed. That her eyes turned from grey to yellow. And that sometimes, in the dark—'

'They gleamed,' Bernie whispered. 'I saw them, Aunt Sheila. They shone in the dark, and they moved—like real eyes.'

'That's exactly what Grannie said. She told me it terrified her so much she wanted to give Grizel away. She began to hate Grizel, but she had to keep her—she was the last person to see Ewan alive, you see.'

'Did you ever see her eyes shine like that?' Bernie asked. 'Did your mother?'

'Never.' Aunt Sheila pushed back her chair. 'There are lots of things you can't explain. I think I'll shut Grizel up in that box from now on. Grannie made me promise never to give her away, so I have to keep her, even though she gives me the creeps—I just won't let her out.' She laughed. 'Listen to me, I'm talking as if she's real.'

'Her eyes are,' Bernie whispered.

'That's so hard to believe,' Aunt Sheila said gently. 'Sometimes I think that it's just your—and Grannie's— overactive imagination. But I'm a much more down-to-earth person than you are. Michelle's like me—but you're different. Maybe you see things that we can't.' She hugged Bernie. 'Let's go and join the others and forget about Grizel. Can you try to stop thinking about her?'

Bernie nodded, but she knew it was impossible.

For the rest of the week, as she travelled around the city with her sister and aunt, Grizel's feverish eyes glittered inside Bernie's brain. They seemed to be asking something of her.

Finally, Bernie gave in. One afternoon, when Aunt Sheila had taken Michelle to get her hair cut, Bernie crept down to the basement.

She carried the cardboard box upstairs so she wouldn't have to open it in the dark. Placing it on the table in the sunny kitchen, Bernie prised open the flaps and unwrapped the towel.

Grizel looked ordinary again—at least, as ordinary as she could with those eerie eyes. But they just reflected the light like any glass eyes.

Bernie lifted the doll out and examined her. She *was* beautiful —no wonder Margaret and Ewan had pretended she was a princess. Grizel's dark hair was as soft as real hair and her long fingers were so carefully modelled.

But Bernie remembered how Grizel's eyes looked in the darkness. She started to put the doll back into the box. But as she closed the flaps the golden eyes seemed to implore her.

Bernie took her out again and held her on her lap, careful not to bang her porcelain arms and legs together. The middle part of Grizel was made of cloth, stuffed with something firm; she made a nice weight.

It wasn't Grizel's fault that her eyes reflected such horror. It was because of what she had *seen*, what she had witnessed as she sat, trapped, on the shelf in the room full of flames. And she hadn't been able to close her eyes, like a human could. A doll had to keep looking.

Bernie shivered and held Grizel closer. Margaret had come to hate her, Aunt Sheila said—as if Grizel represented Ewan's suffering. What a lot to bear—she was only a doll!

Only a doll . . . Bernie hugged Grizel harder as she made up her mind.

What if she began to *play* with Grizel, as her former owners had played with her? Dolls weren't meant to be hated—they were meant to be taken care of, to be dressed and groomed and talked to. Maybe Grizel could become a real doll again—maybe her eyes would even forget what they had witnessed.

I can do it as long as it's daytime, Bernie decided. She could shut Grizel into the box every night. But in the daytime—right now!—she could treat Grizel like an ordinary doll.

Aunt Sheila and Michelle were surprised to find Bernie sitting in the kitchen and doing what everyone does with a doll— brushing her hair.

Now Grizel was with Bernie every moment until bedtime. Bernie combed and braided her hair and tied it with ribbons. She sorted out all the clothes from the other dolls that would fit Grizel and changed her outfit every day. She found some shiny material in Aunt Sheila's sewing-box and made Grizel a cape. With her allowance she went to a handicraft shop and bought sequins for the cape and fake rhinestones that she glued on to a cardboard crown.

'Princess Grizel,' Bernie called her. She made necklaces for her out of a bead kit and yearned for a toy horse on wheels she had at home; it would be just the right size for Grizel to ride on.

Bernie took Grizel everywhere she went, even to Victoria on the ferry.

'You're too old to play with dolls,' Michelle said.

'No, I'm not,' said Bernie, surprising herself with her confidence. 'Aunt Sheila said our great-grandmother played with dolls when she was twelve. And Jennifer likes her.'

It was true. Jennifer came over almost every day, and she began to help Bernie make things for Grizel. By the end of the week even Michelle was giving them ideas for their map of Eleuria. Aunt Sheila became involved, too. They spent their evenings making up names for the members of the royal household. Aunt Sheila said they could paint her old doll's bed so that it was fit for a princess. It rained for three whole days, but none of them cared—they were immersed in an enchanted world that revolved around Princess Grizel.

Only at night was Grizel banished. At first Bernie left her in the box in the kitchen. Then she took the box up to her room, so Grizel would at least be near. But she always closed the flaps.

'Your parents are arriving on Sunday,' Aunt Sheila reminded them one afternoon.

'Already?' said Michelle.

They were sitting on the floor making papier-mâché cups and plates for Grizel. When they were dry they would paint them gold.

But now Michelle put down her cup as if it repulsed her. 'This is so boring,' she said. 'Can't we go to the shops, Aunt Sheila? I'd like to buy that ring I saw so I can show it to Mum.'

'I suppose so.' Aunt Sheila added more paste to her bowl.

'Want to come, Bernie?'

Bernie pretended not to hear. It was as if a spell had been broken. She picked up Grizel and re-tied the bow on her cape. 'There,' she said. 'Now you're ready to receive the ambassador of Eleuria.' But Michelle and Aunt Sheila and Jennifer were already getting ready to go.

'Mum and Dad are going to be surprised you're playing with dolls,' Michelle said that evening.

'I don't care. Anyway, you played with her, too.'

Michelle reddened. 'I wasn't really playing. I was just going along with you because there was nothing else to do. I think you're acting really strange about that doll, Bernie. She's only a doll—you're obsessed with her.'

'I know she's only a doll,' Bernie said. 'It's just a game, but I like it. I *like* pretending things.'

Michelle shrugged. 'Suit yourself.' She got into bed.

Bernie was pleased. She'd said what she thought and Michelle accepted it. Could it be that easy? Could she simply refuse to agree with Michelle if she didn't want to?

I can do what I want! she thought in wonder. For the past week she had, and she'd been so successful that she'd enticed Michelle and Jennifer, and even Aunt Sheila, into her game. She'd thought it was Grizel who had put a spell over them, but it was *her*, Bernie . . .

She gazed at Grizel as she put her in her box for the night. She was only a doll. Only a human, like herself, could make her seem real.

Bernie looked at her and saw—but she knew it was her imagination that saw—how lonely Grizel looked. Despite being groomed and taken on outings and dressed and worshipped and imagined in all sorts of stories about Eleuria, she didn't like going into exile every night. Imagine a princess being shut up in a cardboard box!

Bernie took her out and tucked her into the bed she'd painted. But even there Grizel's amber eyes yearned.

What did dolls like? To sleep beside their owners, of course. To be cuddled in a nice warm bed and whispered to in the dark. That's what Bernie had done with the dolls she used to play with.

But the eyes . . .

Her eyes were like that because my great-grandmother hated her, Bernie thought. Now someone loves her—I do. Now she's a real doll again, with eyes that are ordinary glass.

Despite her beating heart, she undid Grizel's cape, took off her dress, and put one of the other dolls' nightgowns on her. When Aunt Sheila came up to kiss them goodnight Grizel was tucked up beside Bernie.

'Good for you,' Aunt Sheila said, smiling. 'You're not afraid of her at all any more, are you? Just be careful not to roll on her.'

'Imagine still sleeping with a doll,' Michelle scoffed, but Bernie just turned her back and hugged Grizel.

She caught a faint whiff of smoke—but surely that was her imagination. 'Go to sleep,' she whispered.

Bernie turned over and felt one of Grizel's stiff arms jabbing her side. She woke up at once—had she lain on the doll's arm and broken it? She picked Grizel up and felt her arm in the darkness.

The eyes—they glittered and blazed and seethed with fire. Bernie gasped and dropped Grizel on the quilt.

But some new strength made her pick the doll up again. Something made her clutch Grizel and stare into her eyes.

The eyes danced with leaping flames. The eyes crackled with fright and shock and horror. Bernie's whole body shook as she saw what Grizel saw.

Flames licking at a little boy's clothes and then at the flesh of his face and hands. Screams that turned to chokes and then to silence as the small body gave in to the fierce heat of the fire. Smell of scorched clothes and something far worse—scorched flesh.

Bernie hung on to the doll. She wanted to close her eyes but she couldn't—because Grizel hadn't been able to. She was caught in the doll's witnessing of a senseless, monstrous accident. Part of her wanted to fling the horror away, to throw Grizel out of her bed, but she continued to clutch her and watch, too appalled to utter a sound.

And then she knew something else—she knew that Margaret had witnessed the fire as well. That she *had* been able to get into the room but had been too terrified to do anything. That

she'd stood, paralysed with fright, and watched her brother burn to death—and then she had turned to run for help and had fainted outside the door.

Margaret had seen what no one should have to see, and she had never told anyone. She'd held that horror inside her for the rest of her life. That was why she hated Grizel yet couldn't give her away. She kept the doll to torment herself with her guilt.

Finally it was over. The flames died out in the eyes and they became as dim as the rest of the doll's features. Bernie pulled Grizel close to her. 'It's not your fault,' she whispered. 'You couldn't help it. You would have been burned yourself if you'd gone to him. There was nothing you could do.'

She fell asleep cradling Grizel and Margaret.

'Where did you get that beautiful doll?' Mum asked, after all the exclamations and hugs and kisses were over and they were waiting for the luggage to appear.

Grizel had worn her best cape for going to the airport. 'She was Aunt Sheila's—but she just told me I could have her!' Bernie said proudly.

Mum held Grizel. 'What gorgeous grey eyes—they look right at you, don't they?'

'Grey?' Michelle said.

'Let me see.' Aunt Sheila took Grizel. 'Why, look—her eyes aren't yellow any more!'

'Weird,' Michelle said. 'Did you paint them or something, Bernie?'

Bernie just smiled as she claimed Grizel back. 'Her eyes were always this colour,' she said softly. 'You just didn't look at them the right way.'

The Water Mill

ALISON PRINCE

Emma was in the city again. Tall buildings on either side, too high to see the sky, and sloping concrete banks set with lumpy stones so no one could walk on them—not that anyone was trying to walk, only Emma, alone as always in this traffic-roaring place. Where was she going? She didn't know, only that she had to escape. She went through a gap between two buildings but on the other side it was the same, nothing but concrete walls and streets that had no names.

Then the dream shifted, and she was at the water mill, standing on a broad bridge, looking down at a river that poured away over the smooth ledge of a weir. The mill was down there as well, built on rocks where the water rushed through. There were no wheels or machinery that she could see, but inside those white, featureless walls something happened, and when the water came bursting out on the far side it rushed away in a tumbling torrent, newly wild and free. This was the way out from the city.

Emma was hurtling down the river in a frail boat that might be smashed on the rocks at any moment. She was so scared that she could hardly breathe.

KUKK-KURRUKK-KURROOOO!

The mad shriek of Emma's cock-crow watch blasted through the dream. She groped for the button to stop it, then rolled over and lay with the back of her wrist across her eyes. Slowly, the water mill and the running river faded and her thudding heart slackened its pace. This was Saturday morning, August the sixth. Her packed bag stood by the door with her clarinet in its case beside it, together with a music stand Clearly Labelled With Owner's Name. She must get up and be driven to the station, and at the other end a minibus was taking people to the Youth Music Week at Walford Hall.

It was going to be terrible. All the others would be witty and brilliant and good at table tennis. Emma regretted all over again that she'd let her mother talk her into this—but it was so hard to say no. She saw again her mother's anxious face. *But, darling, you'll love it when you get there, I'm sure you will.* So worried, so hopeful. Poor Mum. She'd have liked a daughter who was popular and sporty, rushing around with lots of friends and going out with boys. Someone she could be proud of, in that scandalized way that mothers have.

Emma had never been out with a boy. She thought about it sometimes, but she couldn't see how it was likely to happen. With her pale face and straight, mousy hair, she simply wasn't the kind that boys found interesting. She didn't mind. It was all right, being on her own. Emma turned on her side and scooped up Sarah Jane, the dilapidated rag doll who had been there ever since she could remember. She cuddled her close, treasuring these last moments of not being on the way to Walford Hall, then heard her mother tap on the door.

'Emma? Ten to eight, darling—time to get up.'

A woman with a cardboard notice that said WALFORD MUSIC WEEK stood on the station platform with various musicians already grouped round her. By the shape of the instrument cases,

Emma saw that one was a cellist and several others played violins. There were a couple of trombonists, and a sandy-haired boy with a French horn smiled at her. Emma smiled back gratefully. Most of the others were chatting away as if they'd known each other for years, which was rather what she had expected.

In the minibus, one of the violinists sat beside Emma, but talked to string-player friends across the gangway all the time. Emma stared out of the window as the bus made its way through the busy streets. After a few minutes, it went over a bridge with a river running below, and the dream stood sharply in her mind again. Emma gave her head a small shake. This was different, she told herself. The river was flowing towards her, not away as it did in the dream, and there was no water mill and no tumbling fall between rocks. The water slid calmly beside a towpath where people walked in the shade of willow trees. Yet Emma felt, as she always did in the dream, locked away in a quiet, lonely sadness.

Leaving the town behind, the bus ran between stone-walled fields with cattle or sheep in them, and past an occasional pub with hanging baskets of flowers outside. Then it turned down a tree-lined drive that led through a shadowy bit of woodland, and stopped outside the front door of a slightly dilapidated-looking mansion where rows of cars were parked. This was it, then, Emma thought, as everyone started getting out. Walford Hall. For a whole week.

When Emma found her room, a girl with short fair hair was already in it, taking off her denim jacket. 'Hi,' she said as Emma came in. 'I'm Lindsey. Which bed d'you want?'

'I don't mind,' said Emma, though she'd have liked to be by the window, where she could look out and pretend to be somewhere else.

'I'll go by the window, then,' said Lindsey, heaving her bag on to the bed and unzipping it. 'What do you play?'

'Clarinet,' said Emma, and added, 'What about you?'

'Flute,' said Lindsey. She hauled a battered-looking, once-white woolly rabbit out of her bag and sat him on her bedside table, then glanced at Emma and said, 'Don't laugh. He's called Victor. I take him everywhere—he's for good luck.'

Emma produced Sarah Jane, and it was Lindsey who laughed. 'You're as batty as me,' she said. 'Have you been here before?'

'No,' said Emma.

'Neither have I,' said Lindsey. 'I don't know what we're in for. Still, it should be fun.'

'I hope so,' said Emma. She was feeling quite a bit better.

In fact, the course turned out to be great. Emma was a good sight-reader, so she could hold her own with no problems in the small instrumental groups, and even found herself helping other people when it came to tricky bits of timing. After playing through a wind quintet, the horn player who had smiled at Emma at the station caught up with her on the way to the dining room. She knew now that his name was Paul.

'Are you going to do music as a career?' he asked.

Emma blushed and said, 'I'm not good enough.'

''Course you are,' said Paul. 'What are you, Grade Seven?'

'Six,' said Emma. 'I'm taking seven next term.'

'There you are, then.' And they fell into amazingly easy conversation, until they were joined by a trombonist who wanted Paul to play in a jazz quartet.

Emma found afterwards that she treasured every word.

That afternoon, following the orchestra session, Emma had a free period which she usually spent in practice—but playing so much had begun to make the inside of her lower lip sore, so she decided to give it a rest. She went outside and walked along the stone terrace, glad to be in the fresh air. On the other side of the balustrade, occasional clumps of nettles grew among the phlox and the scented tobacco plants, and the banks that sloped down to mown lawns were feathery with seeding grass. Emma liked these imperfections; they made Walford Hall seem comfortable and friendly.

Skirting the lawns, she went on up a roughly mown slope to the woodland that bordered the grounds, and walked through grassy glades between big old trees and sprawling rhododendron bushes. The sound of a brass band rehearsing came faintly from the house, but she could still hear the quick rustle as a squirrel ran up a tree and sat on a branch, flicking its tail and chattering. The woods grew thicker, shutting out the sun but for sparkles of light—and quite suddenly Emma came to the edge of a lake, fringed with reeds and long grass.

How weird, she thought, to find water up here at the top of the slope. Was it some sort of reservoir, supplying water to the house? She hoped not—nobody could fancy drinking this greenish, weedy stuff. She made her way along the water's edge, treading carefully through the damp grass and feeling wetness squeeze up from the boggy ground round her sandalled feet, and came to a barred grating, half choked with leaves, where the water from the lake poured away underground.

Emma stared at it, fascinated. Where did it go? Somehow, she hated to think that it vanished for good into that darkness under the earth—she wanted to see it come out again somewhere, sparkling and free. She started to work her way down the slope, following as near as she could guess the line of the hidden water that ran in its pipe below the ground. Emerging from the wood, she skirted past the far side of the bowling green and walked down the steps of the sunken rose garden and out the other side. She crossed a path and came to a low stone wall. She leaned over it, looking down at the meadow beyond it—and there was the stream again, wandering between shallow green banks where sheep cropped the grass in the afternoon sun.

The satisfaction of finding it again was tremendous. Emma gave a little sigh of happiness; but in that unguarded moment, a faint shadow of the dream mingled with what she was seeing— some notion of the water having to go through the darkness, through some underground mill that nobody could see, before it was free to go sparkling on its way. She frowned, annoyed by the intrusion of this idea. How much longer did she have to put up with this stupid dream? She wanted to be free of it now, as the stream was free of the imprisoning earth. She glanced at her watch. Nearly tea-break time. She turned and made her way back to the house.

A door at the back of the house, just by the staircase that led up to Emma's room, opened onto a terrace that led directly to the sloping grass and the woodland, and Emma went several times to the lake, to stare at the water that gushed away through the bars of the leaf-choked grating. It invited a game of Pooh-sticks, the dropping in of a twig then a race to see it come out the other end—but she'd never get down the hill quickly enough, Emma told herself. And anyway, games like that were for kids, and she wasn't a kid any more, was she? When she shut her eyes these days, it was Paul she saw, with the floppy cow-lick of hair that fell across one eye. It wasn't just sandy, it was a pinky-gold colour that seemed to shine out at her from across the crowded dining room or from behind the music stands in Orchestra.

Towards the end of the week, things got so busy that there was no time for wandering about outside. Frantic rehearsals were taking place for end-of-course concerts, and before Emma knew it, Friday night had arrived and she was putting on the long skirt and black top her mother had insisted she must bring. *You'll need something pretty, darling, there's bound to be a dance or something.* And she'd been right about that.

To the disgust of the more sophisticated, the dance after the concert was to the music of a scratch folk-band—but Emma enjoyed it. There was none of that awful business of sitting around with a Coke, pretending you weren't interested in dancing anyway. Everyone was grabbed and pushed into a set, and once you knew the routine, it was great to be part of a moving pattern, linking arms, swinging, moving from partner to partner.

At the end of the evening, Emma was standing beside Paul, and he kissed her. Everyone was hugging and kissing, so it was no big deal perhaps, but she went up to her room dizzy and excited.

Lindsey said, 'It's been a great week, hasn't it?'

'Brilliant,' said Emma.

Regretfully, she started to take her clothes out of the little bedside wardrobe and push them into her bag to save time in the morning. Her happiness was giving way to dismay. After tomorrow, there would be no more easy company, no more music except the daily practice. No more Paul. Lindsey was chattering about her plans for next term after she'd been on holiday to Greece with her parents, but Emma couldn't find much to say.

'Well—better get some sleep, I suppose,' said Lindsey. She put her bedside light out and cuddled down and, as usual, was snoring gently almost at once.

Emma lay in the dark with Sarah Jane clutched close, wishing that things could change and be less anxious. Perhaps she was the one who must change. Change . . . She drifted into sleep.

Her feet were icy cold.

Emma woke with a gasp, and as she became aware of her surroundings she gasped again, with a long, terrified shudder which seemed almost to stop her heart. She was standing ankle-deep in the lake. Above her, the moon sailed between drifting clouds, but the trees all round were black-shadowed. How had she come here through this darkness? While still asleep, her mindless body had made its way over the damp grass and

between bushes, ducked without her knowing it under the branches of trees and then started on its weird way through the green water of the lake.

Breathless with the shock of it, Emma paddled her way to the bank, hugging herself in her cotton nightie. Her teeth chattered and she shivered uncontrollably in the chill night air. She made her way back to the house, and found that the door at the foot of the stairs to her room, although of the push-bar emergency kind, had not quite latched itself. This was the way she had come out, then.

She was still shivering when she reached her room and crept into bed. Badly in need of comfort, she reached for Sarah Jane—but the rag doll was not there. Emma groped under her pillow and across the floor, not wanting to put the light on in case she woke Lindsey, but her hands met emptiness. A terrible suspicion grew that she must have taken Sarah Jane with her on this strange, unknowing walk, and left her up there in the damp darkness. Perhaps she should go out again and look for her . . . but Emma's chilled feet were growing warm, and her body was slackening into sleep.

KUKK-KURRUKK-KURROOOO!

'That's a hellish noise,' Lindsey mumbled. 'Don't know how you can live with it.'

Emma located her watch and stopped the crowing. 'Present from Mum,' she said. 'She likes cheerful things.' Then she remembered, and looked round for Sarah Jane, in case the whole thing had been a dream. But the rag doll wasn't there, and when Emma slid a foot out from under the duvet, she saw that it was stained with earth and grass. She gathered up her clothes and bolted along the corridor to the showers.

When she came back, Lindsey was dressed and asked, 'Coming down to breakfast?'

'Um—I just want some fresh air first,' said Emma, and went out again before Lindsey could ask why.

By the lake, Emma searched desperately, but could find no sign of Sarah Jane. In despair, she stood at the lake's edge where she had stood in the night's darkness, and stared across the shadowed water. Then, among the leaves and twigs caught in the bars of the grating, she saw something pale. She ran to the concrete slab that lay across the top of the grating, and stared down. The sodden mass that had been Sarah Jane drifted face down, the bald gaps between its rug-wool hair showing as white streaks. Emma found a stick and prodded the rag doll along to the grass where she could reach it, then, careless of the water that soaked through her sandals she fished out the water-logged, unhuggable Sarah Jane. The stitched pale blue eyes stared up, but the seam along one arm had burst, and so had a foot.

Emma tried to wring the rag doll out, but the kapok stuffing had gone shapeless, pushing its way like thick porridge through the split seams and leaving the main part of the doll as no more than an empty, weed-bedraggled bit of cloth. Even as a part of her mind was frantically thinking of a plastic bag and a faint hope of dreaming up some excuse which her mother would believe, Emma knew this was the end, and she wept for something that would never return.

Using the stick and her hands, she dug a grave in the moist, black earth. She laid Sarah Jane in it and covered her gently, then planted the stick at her head as a marker. 'I won't forget you,' she promised. 'Not ever.' Then she washed her hands in the lake and went back to the house.

In the crowded dining room, Paul looked up and waved, indicating an empty seat beside him. Emma joined him, and Lindsey, sitting opposite, said through a mouthful of toast, 'Enjoy your walk?' Then she saw Emma's tear-stained face, and looked upset herself. 'Awful, isn't it,' she said. 'Such a great week, and now it's all over.'

Emma nodded wordlessly, and Paul put his arm round her shoulders.

On the way to the station, the minibus went over the same bridge, but Emma, with Paul beside her, was on the other side of the road, looking down at water that ran downstream and slid smoothly over a weir. On the bank was a low, white building.

'It used to be a water mill,' Paul said, following her gaze. 'They say it's an arts centre now.'

Emma smiled. 'It would be,' she said as the dream thinned

and faded, changing into something new. *Sarah Jane has gone*, she would say to her mother. And if she did not want to, she need not explain.

Paul was catching the same train, because he came from London, too, only a bus ride from where Emma lived. 'We'll have time for a coffee at the station,' he said.

'Brilliant,' said Emma, and put her hand in his as the minibus went on through the town, leaving the dream and the water mill behind.

Gone

SUE WELFORD

'I haven't really got to have *this* room, have I?' Justin screwed up his nose at the old-fashioned wallpaper, the peeling paint round the window. The ceiling lamp hung from a cob-webbed cord. He flicked the light switch on but nothing happened. The room stayed gloom-shadowed as if it had something to hide. He shivered. The rest of the house was bad enough but this room was worst of all.

'Why can't Sally have it?' he moaned. 'There's plenty of space for all those Barbie dolls of hers.'

'It just needs cheering up, that's all.' Mum was standing behind him with Jackie, the terrier, in her arms. 'And Sally wants the other room. You said you didn't care which one was yours.'

'Well, I've changed my mind,' Justin sulked.

'Too bad,' Mum said.

Justin stepped across the threshold. He shivered again. The

room was long and narrow and gloomy, especially in the corners where one wall met another. There was a small window at the end. The light from it made hardly any difference.

If ever a room could be sinister, Justin thought, swallowing, suddenly nervous. *This is it.*

'Why did we have to move anyway?' he grumbled. 'The other house was great. All my mates were close by and I could walk to school and mess around in the park whenever I liked.'

'The house will be worth a lot of money when it's done up,' Mum said. 'And we got it dirt cheap.'

'Yeah, I can imagine.' Justin looked around. 'This room gives me the creeps.' He turned to Mum. 'Just think, people could have *died* in here.'

Mum laughed. 'When you live in an old house lots of families must have come and gone. That makes a place interesting.'

Justin snorted. 'Interesting? You've got to be joking.' He pulled at the corner of one of the layers of wallpaper. It came off easily, peeling back like a layer of dead skin. Underneath, the wall was a kind of grey colour. Like a mushroom.

'There you are,' Mum said. 'It comes off easily. You can do it yourself.'

'Thanks,' Justin mumbled. 'It's going to be a really cool way of spending the last week of the holidays.'

Mum laughed and gave him a hug. 'Dad can take you to the DIY store tomorrow so you can choose the paper and paint.'

'Great,' said Justin. 'I was looking forward to dossing around, not painting and decorating.'

'You're always dossing around,' Mum said. 'It'll do you good to do something useful for a change.'

The dog was struggling so she put him down. He hurtled away, down the stairs like a mad thing, claws screeching on the bare boards.

'See,' Justin said. 'Jackie thinks this room stinks too.'

In the hall, Dad was shouting at the removal men. 'The piano goes in the front room! The bookcase here in the hall!'

One of them came clumping up the stairs with Justin's computer in his arms. 'This go in here, son?'

'Oh, yeah, stick it on the floor,' Justin said sulkily. 'Not that I'm going to have a chance to play on it for weeks by the look of it.'

'Right.' Justin's dad dumped a bag full of rolls of wallpaper on the floor. Justin came behind with a tin of paint, brushes, sandpaper, scraper, dustpan and brush. He felt bleary eyed and tired.

'Get all the old stuff off first.' Dad went and pulled some more off. A long strip that looked like a serpent when he chucked it on the floor. 'This yellow paper and blue paint will look great.' He slapped Justin on the back and grinned. 'See you later, son.'

Justin sighed. He still hated the room. Even with the sun shining outside, it carried a sense of disaster. The dark corners looked liked doors into a secret realm and the breeze blowing through the rattly window frame sounded like someone trying to get in.

Or out.

Justin had hardly slept at all. It was bad enough having to sleep on a mattress on the floor but it hadn't been that. It had been the nightmare. Shadowy figures, pale faces at windows, running, fear-stricken, down shadowed corridors. He'd woken in a sweat, his heart beating a wild throb of terror. It had been five minutes past midnight and he'd only dozed after that. Dawn brought a feeling of foreboding that somehow would just not go away.

The terrier was crouched in the doorway.

'Come on, boy.' Justin patted his leg. 'There's nothing to hurt you,' he added unconvincingly. Sensibly, Jackie stayed where he was.

Justin gave another sigh and started ripping off the paper. It came off in satisfying long, damp strips. Somehow the act of tearing it off made him feel better. As if the room was shedding an old skin and would take a new life when it was all gone.

'Mum! Dad! Sally! Come and look at this.' Half an hour later, Justin leaned over the banisters and yelled down the stairs.

Dad appeared. He was still unpacking stuff and looked stressed out. 'What is it?'

'Come and look.'

Underneath the wallpaper someone had painted two people. A man, a woman. Figures with sad, downturned mouths. There had been a third, a child, but someone had rubbed it out. You could just see the outline, faded, hardly more than a shadow.

'Yuk!' Sally commented. 'Aren't they horrible.' One Barbie was tucked under her arm, another was clutched in her hand.

Mum went closer. 'It's been done by a child. The expressions are good, though, aren't they. Quite lifelike.'

'Deathlike, you mean,' Sally said. She stared at the shock of wiry hair on the man's head, his dark brows meeting together. She pushed her glasses up on her nose. 'The lady's crying.'

Justin shivered as a cold wind seemed to pass across his heart.

'I wonder who did it?' Mum was standing back now, viewing the figures as you would a painting in a gallery. 'It'll be rather a shame to cover them up.'

'No, it won't.' Justin swallowed and heard in his head the heart-throb of fear. 'It won't be a shame at all.'

That night, Justin was scared to sleep in case the nightmare came again. He tossed and turned. The mural eyes stared down at him. The light from the outside lamp carved weird shadows across the floor. The wind rattled through the window frame. He thought he heard a child's cry then decided it was only a fox calling into the darkness.

It was after midnight when he suddenly sat up, eyes wide against the gloom. There had been a footstep on the stair. Someone stood in the doorway. A dark, stick-shadow of a person, not moving.

'Mum? Dad? That you?' He flung his arm out for the torch that should have been on the floor beside him.

Only it wasn't.

'Dad? Stop mucking around. What do you want?'

Then the figure started moving towards him and Justin felt a wintry blast of fear turn his stomach to ice. At last his fingers closed over the torch and he snapped it on. A pale face stared back at him, eyes wide and scared, hair standing on end. He gave a little scream, then a laugh of relief. Idiot! It was only his reflection in the mirror propped up against the wall. But when he looked back in the dark doorway the stick figure was moving down the landing towards his sister's room.

Then he blinked and it was gone.

'You were dreaming,' Mum said at the breakfast table. 'You must have been tired out. You worked like a slave getting that wallpaper off and the paintwork sanded down.'

'How could I have been dreaming?' Justin was stuffing down large helpings of bacon and egg while Sally pushed hers around the plate, not eating a thing. 'I wasn't even asleep,' he went on, not liking to say he'd been too scared to sleep. They would only think he was being a wally.

Mum and Dad chuckled when he told them about his reflection and laughed again when they heard about the figure in the doorway. But Justin didn't laugh. He knew it wasn't at all funny.

Sally didn't laugh either.

By evening he had stripped and repainted the windows and skirting board. It looked good, a blue the colour of the ocean. He stood back, satisfied. The room was beginning to look better. Maybe he had been imagining its menace after all.

Sally and one of her dolls came in. Justin had caught her several times staring silently at the figures. 'Haven't you covered him up yet?' she asked.

'Does it look like it?' he said irritably.

'When are you going to?' asked his sister.

'Tomorrow,' he said.

She stared at him, her eyes owl-like behind the lenses of her glasses. 'I wish you'd hurry,' she said.

'I am hurrying. I'll be as glad as you when he's gone.'

'No, you won't,' Sally said going out and not looking over her shoulder once.

'Soon be finished, thank goodness,' Justin said at the breakfast table the following day.

'You've done a good job, son,' Dad said.

Sally was sitting there looking half asleep. She looked pale and tired and ready to burst into tears. 'I keep dreaming about them.'

'Who?' asked Justin.

'Those people in your room.'

Mum looked at her with a worried frown. 'Nightmares?'

Sally shrugged. 'Kind of.'

'It'll be a good job when they're gone,' Dad said.

Later, when Dad had taken Sally out for some fresh air, Justin heard the front doorbell ring. Mum went to answer it. She called up the stairs.

'Justin, come down, we've got a visitor,' Mum called.

When he got there she was in the kitchen making tea.

'It's the vicar,' she hissed. 'He visits everyone who moves into the parish.'

'What does he want?'

'No idea, but the woman next door told me he knows everything about everybody apparently.'

'Oh,' Justin said.

'For goodness sake be polite.' Mum pushed past with a tray. 'And try to think of something intelligent to say.'

The vicar was standing with his back to the door gazing at a photograph of Sally on the mantelpiece. He was young and dark haired, wearing jeans and a T-shirt. Not at all what Justin expected.

'Hi.' Justin shuffled his feet in the doorway. Mum introduced Justin and they sat down. Justin fiddled with his fingers. What on earth did you say to a vicar?

But once the man started you couldn't get a word in anyway so he just sat there, listening.

'This is such a nice house,' the vicar said, gazing around. 'In spite of its history.'

Mum looked surprised. 'History? What do you mean?'

'Well . . .' The man started telling them about a family who lived there years ago. Justin's attention drifted but his ears pricked up when he heard the word 'murder'.

'The parents said someone broke into the house and murdered her but no one was ever convicted. General opinion was, though, that the father had killed her.'

'Killed who?' Justin came back with a bump.

'Their little girl,' the vicar said. 'The one who disappeared.'

'How ghastly.' Mum looked shocked and horrified.

'Yes, he was a violent man apparently.' The vicar took a sip of tea and a bite of the shortbread biscuit Mum had insisted he took from the plate. He leaned forward. 'A terrible temper.'

'That doesn't make him a murderer,' Justin said, not really knowing why he should defend the man.

'No, of course not. But apparently the child and the mother were often seen with bruises. And the child was seen staring out of one of the upstairs windows for days on end. Poor mite.'

'Why didn't someone do something about it?' asked Justin's mum.

The vicar shrugged. 'You know what people are like. They don't want to get involved. There was a huge police investigation but nothing ever came of it. Before my time, of course.'

'What happened to the parents?' Justin asked.

The vicar shrugged. 'Moved away apparently. Strangely enough, though, no one has ever lived in this house for very long since it happened. It's changed hands three times since I've been here.'

'Mum and Dad got it dirt cheap,' Justin said.

'Most people do. Everyone who lives here seems to have bad luck.'

'It must be those people on the wall,' Justin said suddenly. 'They're enough to bring anybody bad luck.'

'On the wall?' The vicar looked puzzled.

Mum explained about the painting. 'Would you like to see it?' she enquired.

'I would indeed.' The vicar placed his cup on the table and got up.

Justin led the way.

When the vicar saw the figures he drew in his breath. 'Oh!' His Adam's apple bounced up and down as he swallowed. 'I wonder who they are?'

'Could be anybody,' Justin said.

'Yes,' the vicar murmured. 'Anybody.'

All afternoon, Justin worked like a demon. He wished Dad was there to help out but he was busy trying to sort out his tool shed. Mum was busy too and Sally would only have got in the way. His sister was being a real pain lately, mooching and moaning around the house. She'd had a crying fit the night before, sobbing and refusing to go to bed. She had been allowed in their parent's bed until she had fallen asleep. Then Dad had carried her back to her own room where she had woken once, screaming in the night, but had fallen back to sleep as soon as Mum hurried in.

'She'll soon settle,' Dad had said confidently. 'Moving house is very traumatic.' He had chuckled. 'The third most stressful thing after death and divorce.'

Justin stood back to look. He'd worked from one corner and

covered up the woman and the shadow child. Soon the staring man would go too and jolly good riddance to them all.

'Is Sally with you?' It was lunch-time the following day when Mum came into Justin's room.

'No. I thought she went out with Dad again.' He had seen them from the window, going down the front path and out of the gate.

'They got back about an hour ago. Last time I saw her she was in here staring at what was left of the painting while you were downstairs mixing up some more paste,' Mum said.

Justin shrugged. 'She wasn't here when I came back up.'

Mum went outside to ask Dad. He shook his head too. 'I thought she was with you.'

Justin could hear them calling her all over the house. Calling and calling as if there were a hundred rooms she might be in.

'Maybe she's gone down the shop?' Justin said downstairs.

Mum looked ready to burst into tears.

'She wouldn't have, not by herself. She knows she's not allowed.'

'Well she must be *somewhere*,' Justin said.

But Sally wasn't anywhere. They looked all over. In the garden, down the street, called in at neighbours just in case, phoned friends near their old house to find out if she had made her way there. No one had seen her.

'She's gone,' Mum sobbed. 'Gone.'

Dad called the police.

While they were waiting, Justin sat in Sally's room trying to work out where she might have gone. There was a gap in the row of Barbie dolls lined up on top of her bookcase. Wherever she was, she had got one with her.

A policewoman came and took all the details. 'Now try not to worry,' she said as she left. 'She could have wandered off and fallen asleep somewhere. We'll get on to it right away.'

But they couldn't help worrying. By the time darkness fell they all felt frantic. Mum was in tears. Dad too although he tried not to show it.

Upstairs, Justin sat on his mattress staring at the wall. He tried not to think about all the terrible things that might have happened to his sister. It was just crazy. How could she simply disappear in broad daylight? He could feel the man's eyes boring into the back of his head. Something seemed to draw him round.

Like someone in a nightmare, he got up and went closer. He started to tremble uncontrollably, jerking like someone having a seizure. The man was smiling, a broad, dark sinister smile. The rubbed out child had come through the wallpaper. He could see it clearly. A little girl about Sally's age. She was wearing blue jeans and a white top. She was carrying a doll. It wore a black micro-skirt and high-heeled sandals. Its long blonde hair trailing over the little girl's stick-arm like dead lilies.

A sob came from Justin's throat.

The doll looked just like Barbie.

And the girl, dark haired, brown eyed behind childishly drawn wire-framed glasses looked just . . . like . . .

His heart turned with terror as his mum's words echoed in his ears. '*She's gone . . . gone.*'

Downstairs, Jackie the terrier howled.

Dark Zone

ED WILLIAMS

Lisa was behind Professor Norman when he stopped near the centre of the cavern and turned to their Mexican guide. '*Aquí?*'

'*Bueno*. This place is good.'

Professor Norman put his halogen lamp on the chamber floor and unslung his backpack. 'OK, folks, I want you to spread out, put some space between yourselves, and find a reasonably comfortable place to sit.'

The footing was uneven and treacherously slick. Lisa chose a spot near a stalagmite, by the shallow stream. She was holding together very well, she thought. Claustrophobia tried to grab her only in the narrower passages and, a revelation, the physical movement of walking and climbing seemed to help. She was proud of herself, and proud that no one else in the class suspected the fear she harboured before they started the descent.

Professor Norman sat cross-legged beside the lamp. 'Everybody set? Whatever you do during our little demonstration, don't try to stand up or move around until I tell you.'

He touched the lamp and the light fled into blackness, tearing Lisa's breath away with it. Her hands clenched, fingernails skidded over clammy rock. Fading after-images, monstrous, amorphous shapes, loomed before her.

'Spooky sensation, isn't it?' Professor Norman's voice caromed off limestone walls. Lisa thought she faced him, but was no longer certain of the sound's direction. Her lungs found the damp air again, drank it quick and short.

'We're about two hundred metres deep now, deep enough to swallow a six-storey building, and in the third and final zone of the cave.'

His voice died slowly, in echoes. Lisa heard classmates near her breathe, heard mineral-laden water drip from the travertine, heard the stream moving slowly at her back. Someone shifted with the rustle of a nylon jacket. Her clothes smelled of hours-old bat guano, smeared on as she slid over rocks. It was acrid and metallic, loam and clay mashed into diluted ammonia. But the blackness was thick with moisture, dulling the odour. She shivered.

'This is the dark zone. It is perpetually without light, has no seasonal changes, no naturally occurring air currents, and maintains a constant relative humidity near one hundred per cent.'

She turned her head side to side, listening, seeking orientation. She felt dizzy. Her hands were flat against the cold limestone, reassurance that she could identify *down*.

'Even though bats and larger animals don't venture down here, the dark zone is far from lifeless. The most famous inhabitant is a blind cave fish found only here in Mexico. Its eye sockets are vestigial and overgrown with skin, but its teeth are perfectly functional. The fish is a close cousin of the piranha.'

Lisa flinched. The stream sounded uncomfortably close.

'In fact, the dark zone is home to hundreds of unique species of fish, crayfish, salamanders, beetles, millipedes, and spiders.'

The blackness pressed against her, palpable. She was sure that if she leaned forward her face would touch it, be enveloped by it, suffocated by it—by a sticky, viscous grease alive with crawling, biting, stinging things. A needle of panic trilled her spine.

'These animals have long antennae, or feelers, to compensate for their lack of eyes. They subsist on food that is washed in by streams, or on nutrients in bat droppings or, in some cases, on each other.'

Lisa thought she felt a feathery brush against her right wrist. She jerked her hand up, shifted to her left.

'OK. Enough fun,' said Professor Norman. 'Everybody, cover your eyes. This lamp's going to be painfully bright at first.'

Something bumped her, not from the side or back, but from below. She heard glass shatter. Professor Norman's voice: 'Dammit!'

The cavern groaned. The floor began to tremble, to buckle. Lisa's left hand slipped. She fell on her elbow, hard. Maybe hard enough to break bone.

She realized the others were screaming.

The Corpse Will Walk

CAROLYN SWIFT

The rain spattered against the carriage window as the train pulled out of Heuston Station, but it made no difference to Nora. The engineering works at Inchicore would have been blurred in any case. When her mother had offered her the window seat so she would be able to see the new lambs in the fields as they passed she had been glad, but not because of the lambs. It gave her an excuse to keep her head turned away from the others.

'He was 84,' her mother had said, 'and no one lives for ever. He'd had a good life and died peacefully in his sleep. Sure, wasn't it a grand way to go? He'd have hated to be tied to his bed and a burden on us all, so there's no call to be crying. Look at me! He was my father and I'm not crying.'

All Nora could think of was that this time when they got to Athenry there would be no Granda to meet them, his blue eyes twinkling and the white hair around the back of his head fluffed up like a robin's feathers on a wet day. He may have been her mother's Dadda, Nora thought, but he got on much better with her. She thought of how the two of them would be off in a twinkling across the fields in search of mushrooms or fraughan as her mother called after him, 'Really, Dad, you're worse than she is!'

There would be no more stories now about the strange things that had happened to him or to 'a woman I know' or to 'a man from a neighbouring parish'. Some of the stories were scary, too, about the banshee that wailed amongst the trees whenever one of the Glynns died, or the foxes that gathered around the castle the time the old lord lay on his death bed. Still, sitting round the fire with the smell of the turf smoke twitching her nostrils, it was a nice sort of scary and Nora had never ever thought of Granda himself dying.

As the train stopped with a jerk at Portarlington Station, the smoke from her father's pipe drifted across the carriage in the draught from the open door and made her cough. Immediately she could hear her grandfather's voice, almost as if he were sitting by her side.

'Carry on with the coughin', Nora,' he chuckled, as he always did. 'The corpse'll walk!'

The first time he had said it, she hadn't understood what he meant.

'Don't mind him,' her mother had told her, seeing the puzzled look on her face. 'He must have his little joke. It's a pun on the word "coughing". Carry on with the coffin, the corpse will walk.'

Funny, Nora thought now, how so many of Granda's jokes were to do with death, only now it wasn't funny at all.

'May I have your attention, please! We will shortly be arriving at Athenry Station. Next stop Athenry.'

At the familiar words coming over the train's sound system, Nora could no longer hold back the tears. How excited she had always felt when she heard those words, wondering what surprise her grandfather had for her this time. There might be three little furry kittens hidden away in the straw in the corner of the barn, or maybe a new little calf for her to visit on the farm at the end of the lane. But this time there would be no

Granda with a finger to his lips, pulling her aside to whisper some secret for her ears alone. Clutching her case, she followed her mother down from the train and out of the station to the big black car that was waiting to drive them to Granda's house.

It looked strange with the curtains drawn in the daytime and, even though Aunt Tina came to the gate to meet them, it seemed oddly silent without the sound of Granda's stick, tapping merrily along the flagged path, and his mischievous chuckle as he winked at her to let her know he had something to tell her as soon as her parents were out of the way.

'Come and say goodbye to your Granda,' Aunt Tina said, taking her by the hand and leading her into the parlour.

But inside the long wooden box on the parlour table there was only a grey-faced old man with his eyes closed.

'That's not Granda!' Nora cried.

'Don't be silly,' her mother snapped, but Aunt Tina took her in her arms and kissed her saying, 'True, for your Granda's in heaven now. It's only his corpse that's there.'

Dressed in her best clothes, Nora sat beside Aunt Tina in the car, driving slowly along the road to the church behind the big, black hearse which held the long wooden box, its lid now firmly nailed down.

'Where's Dadda going?' Nora asked, as her father, looking strange in his black tie, left them to join Uncle Matt and his two sons beside the hearse.

'He's going to carry in the coffin,' Aunt Tina explained, and again Nora seemed to hear her grandfather chuckle: 'Carry on with the coughin', the corpse'll walk!'

But though her father carried one corner of the coffin on his shoulder and Uncle Matt and cousins Tom and Pat carried the other three corners, no corpse got out of it and walked, though Nora kept her eyes on it all through the prayers and afterwards, while the people were filing past them, saying how they were sorry for their trouble.

That night Nora tossed and turned in the bed in the little room next to the one that had been her grandfather's. It seemed to her that someone kept tapping on the window, though Aunt Tina said it was only the branches of the old oak tree, blown by the wind that was rising from the west. Only when Aunt Tina put a small night-light on the little table beside her bed, so Nora could see that nothing lurked in the shadows behind the wardrobe, did she finally fall asleep.

She was awakened by a strange rumbling sound and the noise of horses' hoofbeats. It was still dark in her room, apart from the tiny pool of faint light around her night-light, but a silvery finger of moonlight poked through the slit between the drawn curtains towards her bed. The hoofbeats seemed to stop right outside her window, as she heard the neighing of the horses, and Nora thought there must be travellers' ponies loose on the road.

Shivering a little, she slid out of bed and went across to the window, pulling aside the right-hand curtain. Then she screamed, a scream so long and piercing that Aunt Tina came running into the room, the grey hair she normally wore in a bun loose around her shoulders. When she saw Nora's white face and staring eyes, the pupils big and dark with fear and her mouth still wide from screaming, she pulled her away from the window and on to her bed, wrapping the old-fashioned quilt around her for warmth.

'What's wrong, pet?' she cried. 'Hush, now, or your poor mother will think you're being murdered in your bed.'

'The Death Coach!' Nora sobbed. 'It's outside the gate now.'

'You only dreamed it, pet,' Aunt Tina soothed. 'I should never have taken you to see your Granda, only the two of you were always such pals I thought you'd want to see the last of him. But 'twas too much of a shock for you and it's given you nightmares.'

'No!' Nora cried. 'I did see it! It was just the way Granda described it. Right outside in the moonlight: a big old coach like the one in the shed at Moylans, with two black horses and a coachman up in front, but the coachman had no head!'

Aunt Tina walked over to the window and drew back the curtain so that bright moonlight flooded the room.

'There's nothing there, pet, I promise you,' she said. 'Come and see for yourself.'

But Nora only pulled the quilt over her head. When Aunt Tina tried to draw her over to the window, she struggled with her, clinging to the bed.

'Maybe *you* can't see it,' she sobbed, 'but it's there. And an

old man with a thin, white, bony face, wearing a long black shroud got out of it and looked straight at me before he turned and sort of glided away.'

'It was a nightmare, pet,' Aunt Tina repeated, 'look!'

And with surprising strength for her mother's elder sister, whom Nora had always thought frail, she forced the struggling, sobbing girl to the window. Nora closed her eyes tight shut, afraid to look. After a while, however, hearing nothing but her aunt's pleas to her to look, she opened her eyes a small chink. The branches of the old oak tree stirred in the strengthening wind but, where only moments ago the coach had stood in the moonlight, now there was nothing but an old cardboard box, blown from heaven knows where.

'You see, pet,' her aunt said gently. 'There's nothing there.'

'But I heard the rumbling of the wheels,' Nora insisted. 'That's what woke me.'

'It was probably thunder,' Aunt Tina told her. 'There's a storm forecast. I thought we'd have had it here before this. Now, be a good girl and get back into bed and I'll bring you up a mug of warm milk that will help you sleep. Heaven only knows we all need a good night's rest before facing into the funeral in the morning.'

'I'd be scared to close my eyes for fear the Death Coach would come back,' Nora said but in the end she did, never opening them again until her mother shook her.

'Hurry, Nora,' she said, 'and get yourself washed and dressed. We've all too much to do this morning to be up and down the stairs calling you.'

The sky was dark and threatening, but the storm Aunt Tina had talked about had still not arrived. Ashamed of having woken her aunt, Nora leaped out of bed, hoping her father and mother knew nothing of what had happened. In this, however, she was disappointed.

'I hope you apologized to Aunt Tina for disturbing her night's sleep,' her mother said to her over breakfast. 'As if she hadn't troubles enough just now.'

'Sure, she couldn't help it,' her aunt cut in, before Nora could say anything. 'She cried out in her sleep. It's no great wonder for she's as upset as the rest of us.'

'Would you believe I never heard a thing?' her father exclaimed, 'but then I supposed I'd be sleeping soundly after the day that was in it.'

'You mean, after all the whiskey you put away,' her mother corrected him, but her father only said, 'Wouldn't the neighbours think badly of me if I hadn't taken a drink or two with them, the way your father would have done?'

The funeral was much like the removal the day before only much, much longer and this time Nora sat dry-eyed, only crying afterwards in the graveyard when they lowered the coffin into the big hole they had opened up against the headstone with her grandmother's name on it. Then they laid a board over the hole, put her little bunch of early primroses on top of it amongst all the wreaths and cut flowers and it was all over. And not a minute too soon either, Nora thought, as the rain that had been threatening all morning started to come down in sheets.

That evening, as they stood on the dimly-lit station platform with the blackness of the night all around them, waiting for the train from Galway, she felt her eyelids drooping. Again the neighbours had come back to the house and she had helped her mother and Aunt Tina to hand round plates of sandwiches and cups of tea, while her father looked after the drinks. Now, as she sat on the little bench, her legs swinging, her eyes began to close.

Suddenly a rumble of thunder jerked her awake. For a moment she was panic-stricken, thinking it was the rumble of the Death Coach returning, until she saw where she was. Then she heard the rumble of the approaching train, as the 6:25 from Galway pulled into the station. The engine went past her up the platform in a whiff of diesel oil, making her cough and once again she thought of her grandfather and his little joke.

'Come along,' her mother said impatiently, making for the door of the carriage right in front of them.

Just as they got to it the door opened and out of it stepped an old man with a thin, white, bony face. He was wearing a long, shapeless black cape and for a moment he looked straight at Nora, before turning and moving off down the platform towards the exit with a strange, gliding walk. With a scream, Nora turned and ran in the opposite direction. Her father hurried after her and caught her by the arm.

'What's wrong with you?' he demanded. 'Have you gone crazy?'

'I'm not getting on that train!' Nora cried.

'Don't be ridiculous,' her father said. 'How am I to get to work in the morning?'

As her mother caught up with them, the guard began slamming the carriage doors shut.

'Hurry up or we'll miss the train!' she shouted.

With that her husband snatched up the struggling Nora in his arms and carried her bodily on to the train, throwing her down into the window seat of the nearest carriage as the guard blew his whistle and the train started to move off.

'Now,' her father said as the train gathered speed, 'perhaps you'll be good enough to tell us what all that nonsense was about?'

'It was like my dream!' Nora sobbed.

'I never heard such rubbish!' her father snapped, but her mother put a hand on his arm.

'How d'you mean, like your dream?' she asked, but Nora seemed unable to explain.

'As if the funeral wasn't bad enough,' her father began, but again his wife cut in.

'Try to be patient with her,' she said. 'It's that has her so upset.'

It was at that moment that they all heard a sudden terrible bellowing and a screeching of brakes. The whole train seemed to shake and Nora found herself flung across the carriage. There was an awful crashing sound, her mother screamed and all the lights in the carriage went out as the train shuddered to a stop.

From the darkness outside, Nora heard a strange confusion of screams, cries, and hurried footsteps. Stumbling to her feet, she peered out of the window, but only a faint flickering light like that of a hand-held torch beam could be seen through the rain-streaked glass. Suddenly there was a flash of lightning and, for a brief second, she saw the tail end of the train on the curve of the track, the last carriages tipped over on their sides like a line of coffins. Then all was darkness and confusion once more, until the sound of approaching sirens drowned the other noises. Someone wrenched open the carriage door.

'Is everyone all right in there?' came a man's voice out of the darkness.

'Yes, thank God!' her mother replied. 'What happened?'

'Cattle on the line at Ballyboggen crossing,' the man said. 'The storm must have scared them into stampeding in front of the engine. The last five carriages are derailed and we've instructions to get all passengers out.'

'It's lashing rain,' her mother protested, reluctant to leave the shelter of the carriage for the storm raging outside.

'They're bringing up buses,' the man said. 'Come on, I'll help you down.'

It was a long drop to the tracks, but Nora's father lifted her down into the arms of the man standing below, who lowered her gently on to the grass beside the track. Struggling with their cases towards the line of waiting buses through the long wet grass, rain slanting into their faces and thunder still rumbling overhead, Nora heard again the bellowing of the injured bullocks. It was like her nightmare all over again, only with thunder in place of the rumbling of the coach wheels and the cries of the cattle instead of the neighing of the horses. Only when they sat shivering on one of the buses, waiting for the last of the uninjured passengers to board, were they able to look back at the scene of the accident, where firemen were trying to free the dead and injured from the twisted metal of the toppled carriages.

Her mother gave Nora an odd look. Then she turned to her father. 'Do you realize we would have been in one of those end carriages if Nora hadn't run off?' she asked.

'True,' her father agreed. 'So maybe we should be thankful for her nonsense after all.'

'It wasn't nonsense,' Nora said. 'I know it now. It was a warning. Granda always said the Death Coach was a warning of death. I think now it was Granda that sent it to me, the way I'd run away and not be killed.'

Her father only smiled but, the more Nora thought about it, the more she felt sure that it was indeed her grandfather that had let her see the likeness of a walking corpse coming from one of the end carriages, carriages that were now like tombs for so many who had travelled in them.

Acknowledgements

Inside illustrations are by:
Martin Cottam: p.27, p.57, p.75, p.78, p.112, p.138, p.143
Paul Fisher Johnson: p.5, p.63, p.72
Ian Miller: p.146, p.153, p.157, p.160, p.201
Brian Pedley: p.11, p.14, p.17, p.41, p.45, p.51, p.84, p.91, p.93, p.95, p.179, p.185, p.189, p.192
Tim Stevens: p.viii, p.29, p.31, p.34, p.102, p.108, p.124, p.164, p.167, p.168, p.177

Kingsley Amis: 'Mason's Life', first published in *The Sunday Times* 1972, from Kingsley Amis: *Collected Short Stories* (Hutchinson, 1980), copyright © 1980 Kingsley Amis, reprinted by permission of the Random House Group and Jonathan Clowes Ltd, London, on behalf of the Literary Estate of Sir Kingsley Amis; **Francis Beckett:** 'Seafood', © Francis Beckett 2000, first published in this collection by permission of the author; **Sydney J. Bounds:** 'Dream Ghost', copyright © Sydney J. Bounds 1976, first published in Mary Danby (ed.): *The Eighth Armada Ghost Book* (Fontana, 1976), reprinted by permission of the author; **Fredric Brown:** 'Nightmare in Blue' from *The Best Short Stories of Fredric Brown* (New English Library, 1982), copyright © the late Fredric Brown, reprinted by permission of A. M. Heath & Co. Ltd; **John Burke:** 'The Lost Child' first published in Herbert van Thal (ed.): *Lie Ten Nights Awake* (Hodder paperbacks 1967), reprinted by permission of Hodder & Stoughton Ltd; **Michael Chislett:** 'The Gargles', © Michael Chislett 2000, first published in this collection by permission of the author; **J. J. Curle:** 'Blood will Cry Out', (originally called 'Awake-Asleep-Awake') first published in R. C. Bull (ed.): *Upon the Midnight* (Macdonald 1957), reprinted by permission of Little, Brown and Company (UK); **Berlie Doherty:** 'Nightmare' first published in Jean Richardson (ed.): *Beware! Beware!* (Hamish Hamilton, 1987), reprinted by permission of David Higham Associates; **Marien Dreyer:** 'The Big Wind', first published in *The New Idea* (Pacific Publications) copyright holder not traced; **John Edgell:** 'Four Twenty-four Precisely' from *John Edgell's Ghosts* (Wayland Publishers, 1970): copyright holder not traced; **Adèle Geras:** 'S. Q.', © Adèle Geras 2000, first published in this collection by permission of the author, c/o Laura Cecil Literary Agency; **John Gordon:** 'Uncle Walter', © John Gordon 2000, first published in this collection by permission of A. P. Watt Ltd on behalf of the author; **Dennis Hamley:** 'Dream Fountain', © Dennis Hamley 2000, first published in this collection by permission of the author; **Kenneth Ireland:** 'Frisky', © Kenneth Ireland 2000, first published in this collection by permission of Jennifer Luithlen on behalf of the author; **Gerald Kersh:** 'The White-Washed Room' from *Men Without Bones* (Heinemann, 1955): copyright holder not traced; **Sheila Lavelle:** 'Scottish Melody', © Sheila Lavelle 2000, first published in this collection by permission of the author; **Christopher Leach:** 'Mrs Beale and Trixie' from *Scars and Other Ceremonies* (J. M. Dent, 1980), reprinted by permission of Orion Publishing Group Ltd; **Morgan Llywelyn:** 'Nightmare', first published in *Nightmares – Terrifying Tales from Beyond the Grave* (Poolbeg Press, 1996), reprinted by permission of the author; **Michelle Magorian:** 'The Front Room', copyright © Michelle Magorian 1983, first published in *They Wait and Other Spine Chillers* (Pepper Press), reprinted by permission of the author, c/o Rogers, Coleridge & White Ltd, 20 Powis Mews, London W11 1JN; **E. W. Mayo:** 'Dream Justice', copyright © Popular Fiction Publishing Co., reprinted by permission of Weird Tales Ltd; **Philip Murray:** 'The Patch' from *Shudders* (Philip Allan, 1932): copyright holder not traced; **Kit Pearson:** 'The Eyes' from *Fingers on the Back of the Neck and Other Spine-Tingling Tales* (Puffin, 1998), reprinted by permission of the author; **Alison Prince:** 'The Water Mill', © Alison Prince 2000, first published in this collection by permission of Jennifer Luithlen on behalf of the author; **Robert Scott:** 'Badnight Story', © Robert Scott 2000, first published in this collection by permission of the author; **Carolyn Swift:** 'The Corpse Will Walk', copyright © Carolyn Swift 1994, from *Shiver!* (Poolbeg, 1994), reprinted by permission of the author; **Sue Welford:** 'Gone', © Sue Welford 2000, first published in this collection by permission of the author; **Ed Williams:** 'Dark Zone', © Ed Williams 1998, first published in Stefan Dziemianiwicz et al (eds.): *Horrors! 365 Scary Stories* (Barnes & Noble, 1998), reprinted by permission of the author.

Despite every effort to trace and contact copyright holders prior to publication, this has not been possible in a few cases. If notified, the publisher will be pleased to rectify any errors or omissions at the earliest opportunity.

Badnight Story

ROBERT SCOTT

She knew it, knew it well, had known it long before Uncle Tim took her to see the mummified corpses. Now, though, she saw it, saw the grinning, lipless face; the hard, blackened skin; the clawed hands with their long, yellow nails as it pursued her, ape-like, through her dreams.

'You should be ashamed!' she had heard her mother storming at Uncle Tim. 'Fancy taking a sensitive young girl like our Mel to a place like that!'

She had crept away, hot with guilt, knowing that she had been the one who wanted to go there. It made no difference now. This creature, this *thing* she had fashioned from the grinning rags and tatters of the long-dead, invaded all her nights.

Its grasping talons clutched at her as she fell endlessly into swirling, bottomless darkness. It pursued her as she stumbled across the clattering railway lines with their clanking wagons and shrieking locomotives. Always terrifying, always closer, it caught at her as she fled in laboured slow-motion through the empty city streets until, at last, she jolted out of her nightmare, panting and sweating, into her familiar bedroom.

Again! And suddenly she was upright, terror surging within her. Each night those dead claws slashed at her. Each night it played with her, feeding on her panic. And tonight . . .

That was when, wide awake now, she switched on her bedside light—and saw the clawed hand reach over the foot of her bed.